MAFIA MARRIAGE TROUBLE

By
Alex McAnders

McAnders Books

Titles by Alex McAnders

M/M Romance

Serious Trouble & Audiobook; Book 2 & Audiobook;
Book 3 & Audiobook; Book 4 & Audiobook; Book 5
Serious Trouble - Graduation Day; Book 2; Book 3;
Book 4
Mafia Marriage Trouble

MMF Romance

Searing Heet: The Copier Room; Hurricane Laine &
Audiobook; Book 2 & Audiobook; Book 3 &
Audiobook; Book 4 & Audiobook; Book 5; Book 6

M/M Wolf Shifter

His Caged Wolf; Book 2; Book 3; Book 4; Book 5
His Wolf Protector

MAFIA MARRIAGE
TROUBLE

Chapter 1

Dillon

I stared at my phone for the hundredth time, willing it to ring. 7:24 pm. Tyler was officially 24 minutes late for our date. I bounced my leg anxiously and chewed my bottom lip unable to quell the sinking feeling in my stomach.

This wasn't like Tyler at all. We had been chatting online for weeks now, and he seemed so sweet, so genuine. I had really thought this could be the start of something real. My heart had fluttered reading Tyler's texts, seeing how considerate he was, how interested in my life and dreams. It gave me hope that maybe, just maybe, I could find a love like my best friend Hil had.

Hil had met his boyfriend Cali so effortlessly, so instantly falling into an easy, loving relationship. Yet here I was, still struggling just to get a first date with a guy I had really connected with online. A guy who seemed to share my feelings and understand what it was like to be young, gay and searching for love.

Everything always seemed so much harder for me – making ends meet, finishing school, finding someone to love me for who I am. Now, here I was sitting alone in the cozy cafe Tyler and I had picked for our first date.

Had I completely misread the signs with Tyler? Was he just looking for a hookup and nothing more? Or worse, had I gotten my hopes up about someone who was just luring me in with empty promises?

I checked my phone again. 7:27 pm. The sinking feeling in my gut twisted sharply. Blinking back tears, I muttered under my breath, "Don't cry, you idiot. It's just a first date."

But it was more than that and I knew it. This date had represented something much bigger – a chance at the true love I desperately wanted. A possibility of having someone finally see me, want me, love me for exactly who I was.

All I had wanted was what seemed to come so easily to everyone else – a loving partner by my side. But disappointment after disappointment was starting to take its toll.

A tear escaped rolling down my cheek when the cafe door chimed open. I quickly brushed it away, feeling foolish. An attractive couple walked in, arm in arm, laughing lightly together. The twist in my gut wrenched tighter. He wasn't coming. And I wasn't even worth a text.

Swallowing, I couldn't bear the thought of going back to my empty apartment tonight with another failure to endlessly agonize over. All I wanted was to know what it felt like to be loved. Was that so much to ask for?

But as the minutes ticked by, the truth set in. I had been foolish to get my hopes up in the first place. So with a deep, shuddering breath, I gathered my jacket and walked out of the cafe alone.

Chapter 2

Remy

I stood in my father's once grand office, now transformed into a makeshift hospice room. Hil and my mother were next to me, all of us looking down at our father's lifeless body. The silence was suffocating, broken only by the soft sobs of my mother trying to hold back her tears.

Heartbreak washed over me. But gazing over the shadows cast on my father's face by the dim light, I felt more than that. His was a mixed legacy. I had spent my life proving my worth to him. I had done things I wasn't proud of. Now that he was gone, I wondered if it had all been for nothing.

Hil broke the silence. "I'll organize the funeral. I want to do this for Father," he said, his voice wavering with emotion. I could tell he was still desperate for our father's approval, even after his death.

I glanced at him, my heart aching for my brother who had tried so hard to escape the life of crime our family had been born into. He hadn't been built for it like I was. Unlike me, he had never been able to hide his attraction to men. It hung around his neck like a scarlet letter. To my father's credit, he never judged Hil for it. But when my father and I were alone, he didn't hide his disappointment.

It wasn't for what Hil wanted to do with other men. It was for what it meant about his ability to thrive in our unforgiving world. People wanted my father dead. Given the way Father claimed his power, I understood why.

But that meant that no one in our family was safe. Hil, and his sensitive nature, would always need someone to keep him alive. Father had no problem in doing that, but it was clear that he wanted a son who could take care of himself.

That was what I became for him. I took care of myself. Always unsure of when the pass he gave Hil would end, I soon took care of Hil too. I didn't mind. He was my little brother. It was my job. But having to be the man my father wanted me to be took its toll.

"Thank you, Hil," I said, my voice betraying the pain I felt.

My mother reached over and squeezed my hand, her touch tingling with a mix of sadness and gratitude. I could see the hope in her eyes for a better future, free from the violence and danger that had plagued our family for so long.

My thoughts drifted to the pact I had made with Armand Clément, my father's most vicious rival. I had agreed to hand over my father's illegal businesses to him in exchange for keeping the legal ones and securing my family's safety.

We would be out of the mafia world, and under his protection. It was a desperate gamble, but I couldn't stand the thought of carrying this on without the immense pressure I had felt from my father to do it.

Besides, our family already had so much to make amends for. At some point, I was going to need to figure out how to give back to the community. Father's obsession with power had caused a lot of pain. That couldn't be my family's only gift to the world.

It was then that Dillon flashed through my mind. He was Hil's best friend and the boy whose presence never let me forget that I wasn't straight. His lean lines, his lightly tanned skin, his loosely curly hair that I dreamed about pushing my fingers through.

They all turned me into a man who dreamed every night about holding him. A guy who fantasized about sliding my hand up his tee shirt and wrapping my large hands around his narrow chest. He was my anchor in my father's turbulent seas and now, the ocean that kept me from Dillon lay in front of me, dead, missed, and regretted.

Excusing myself before my family saw the smile that slowly crept across my face, I headed to my childhood bedroom. I couldn't wait another second. I needed to hear his voice. My heart pounded at the thought. I had to call him.

Retrieving my phone, I found his number. Taking a deep breath, I dialed. My heart pounded in anticipation. The phone rang and my palms grew sweaty.

"Hello?" Dillon's voice came over the line, warm and soothing as always.

"Hey, Dillon, it's Remy." I tried to keep my voice steady as I spoke. "I just wanted to let you know that my father... he passed away."

"Oh, Remy, I'm so sorry." Like all of us, he had known it was coming. But his empathy washed over me like a comforting wave. "How are you holding up?"

My throat tightened as I struggled to maintain my composure. "I'm... managing," I admitted, the weight of my emotions threatening to spill over. Desperate to regain control, I swiftly changed the subject. "Listen, I was wondering if you could help me with something."

"Of course. What is it?"

"Hil said that he wants to make the funeral arrangements. I think he could really use your support right now."

There was a pause on the other end before Dillon softly agreed. "You didn't have to ask that, Remy. I'll do whatever I can to help."

The silence that followed was heavy with unspoken words, my heart aching to tell him the truth about my feelings for him. But I couldn't bring myself to say it, not yet.

"Thanks. I always know I can count on you," I said with a smile.

"It's no problem, Remy. I like being able to help you… and Hil," he reassured me, his voice filled with genuine care. "We'll all get through this together. Just let me know what you need."

I nodded, even though he couldn't see me. "I appreciate it."

"I know," he said assuredly.

As I hung up the phone, I wondered what I was doing. I didn't have to restrain myself to two-minute conversations with him anymore. I was free. I didn't know how he felt about me, but I no longer had to hide my feelings for him. It was time for me to tell him.

Heat washed through me, considering it. It was a mixture of terror and exhilaration.

"After the funeral," I said aloud. "My new life begins at the end of my old one."

I could barely imagine living without hiding and secrets, but here it was. I was going to embrace the truth and see where it would take us. Was being with Dillon really going to be that simple? I didn't know, but I was about to find out.

Chapter 3

Dillon

Ending the call with Remy, I stood in my apartment with my saddle bag still over my shoulder. I had just walked in having returned from being stood up on my date and Remy's had been the first voice I had heard. I could no longer feel my face.

Had Remy just called me? I wondered as my heart raced, washing away the heartbreak of an hour ago. What had been the purpose of his call?

He had said it was to get me to help Hil, but he had to have known I would have done that anyway. No, there had to be more to it than that. Was he seeking comfort for his father's death? Because as much as I have wanted us to be, Remy and I weren't that close.

So, could the reason for his call be something else? Could it be that he was secretly in love with me and that I hadn't been crazy all of these years for dreaming that he was?

It was because of Remy that I had been stood up on my date tonight. Well, not directly because of him. But it was because I had interacted with Remy so much while Hil was missing that I had noticed the gaping hole in my life. Could it have been the same for him?

Thinking about it, I immediately remembered the many reasons Remy would have no interest in someone like me. For starters, although I wasn't normally a complete mess, around him, I was. There were two months after Hil and I became friends where I couldn't even form words in his presence.

I was 14 years old, not 10. And yeah, he was super-hot, even then. But there was no reason I should have lost the ability to speak around him.

Then there was the time Remy caught Hil and me watching gay porn in Hil's room. I had asked Hil if he had locked the door, and he assured me he had. So, when Remy burst in, finding us with our dicks in hand, I could have passed out.

And finally, let's not forget the time when I was 16 and Hil's parents let me stay at their place while Hil's family took my mother on vacation with them. I had school so I couldn't go, but thinking I had the place to myself, I had a one-man naked dance party in their penthouse, complete with towel turban and hairbrush microphone.

Remy chose that moment to come by and check on the place. It wouldn't have been so bad if little Dillon hadn't been so excited to be out. But who could blame the guy? Show me someone who doesn't like to bounce to the beat of 'Bad Romance' and I'll show you someone who doesn't know how to live.

My cheeks burned at the memories. But as I always did, I reminded myself that the humiliation I experienced in front of Remy didn't matter. Because as much as I liked to fantasize about it, a guy like Remy, with his Greek God build, gorgeous hair, and mafia princeling status, couldn't possibly be attracted to guys, much less someone like me.

Besides, this wasn't the time for fantasies. I needed to focus on helping Hil through this difficult time. Despite their complicated relationship, I knew how much he loved his father. Yes, his father had locked him away in their penthouse never allowing Hil to have a social life outside of me. But that wasn't because his father was a monster. They have a dangerous life.

And, it wasn't like his father was wrong. The one time Hil escaped his family's protection, he ended up being kidnapped by one of his father's rivals. Remy and Hil's boyfriend, Cali, had had to rescue him. The guy shot Cali in exchange for letting Hil go. Cali was alright, but still. Hil and Remy lived in a crazy world and his father had had to protect Hil from it.

On the other hand, when it became clear that Hil was gay, his incredibly scary father accepted him for who he was. Hil told me that never once did his father make him feel bad for who he was attracted to. Hell, his parents even introduced the two of us and it wasn't like anyone ever mistook me for straight.

So, despite everything, Hil's father had been a way better dad than mine had ever been. And now his father was gone. My heart ached for him.

Taking a deep breath, I promised myself to set aside any feelings I had for Remy and focus on being there for Hil in the coming weeks. And as the tingles I always got from thinking of Remy subsided, I again picked up my phone.

I wasn't sure why I was nervous, but dialing Hil's number, my heart pounded. When the call connected, Hil's voice was shaky.

"Hey, Dillon."

"Hey, Hil… I just heard about your father."

There was a slight pause. "Really? How?"

"Remy just told me," I said wanting so badly to share how amazing it was that he had.

"Oh. Yeah."

"I'm so sorry, Hil. How are you doing?" I said wishing I could reach through the phone and hug him.

"It's just so hard to accept that he's gone."

"I can't even imagine. But I'm here for you, okay? Whatever you need, I'll be there."

Hil sighed, his voice cracking ever so slightly. "I appreciate that. I told Remy I wanted to handle the funeral."

"Wow, that's a lot."

"Yeah, but I told Cali I was planning to and he asked if he could help me with it. So, I'll be leaning on him for most things."

"That's great."

"Yeah," he said followed by a pause.

"What is it?"

"There is something you can help me with, though."

"Of course! Anything. Just tell me when and where."

The next day, Hil and I found ourselves in a boutique urn store. I didn't even know there wasn't such a thing. But there was and here we were.

The place exuded a somber elegance, with soft lighting casting a warm glow on the polished, hand-painted vessels. Being there, shopping for the last resting place of Hil's father, felt surreal. It was just for the significance of it, it was also for the price tags.

With all due respect, urns were just vases with tops. How could one cost $22,000? Sure, it was marble with adorned gold filigree… whatever that was. But I could barely afford the bus I took here.

As we drifted through the aisles browsing the diamond urn collection, the topic of our conversation shifted from his father to Remy. I wasn't the one who had changed it. But I wasn't about to pass up on an opportunity to add material to my spank-box... when such a thing again became appropriate to do... to the thought of your best friend's brother.

"I think I've come to peace with Father liking Remy best. I mean, I get it. He has my father's need to take care of everyone. He even had it as a kid.

"There were times when we were growing up that he would do the worst big brother crap to me. But if you asked who I thought would protect me if something bad happened, it wouldn't be a question. It would be him."

I nodded, understanding how much Remy meant to Hil. "He's always been there for you, hasn't he?"

"Yeah, but at the same time, I can't help but worry about him."

"Why's that?" I asked, my curiosity piqued.

Hil sighed, running a hand through his hair. "I just don't think he'll ever be able to leave our family life behind."

"And by "your family life" you mean your family's business?

"Yeah. And I know he made the deal that's supposed to free us, but I'm not sure there's any way out."

"You got out," I said referring to Hil's new small-town life with his boyfriend in Tennessee.

"I did, but I was never a part of that world. My father once told Remy and me that the only way to leave a family was in a body bag. I don't think Remy could get out if he tried."

I frowned, not wanting to believe that. "I think with the right person by his side, he could definitely leave that life behind."

Hil glanced at me, his expression unreadable. "Dillon, are you talking about yourself?"

I hesitated, realizing how it must have sounded. "Well, I mean, not just me. But someone who cares about him and wants to see him happy."

Hil shifted uncomfortably, clearly not liking the idea. "Can I ask you a serious question? Because I know you like to joke about things."

"Of course you can. What is it?"

"Do you really think you and Remy…"

As soon as he began saying it, my face felt like it was on fire. I wasn't sure if I was embarrassed or just hurt, but I couldn't take hearing him finish what he was about to say.

"I mean, why not?" I interrupted. "Is it so ridiculous to think that I could be good for him?"

"No, Dillon, it's not that." Hil sighed, his voice strained. "I think he's not good for you. You're the greatest person I know. What if something were to happen between the two of you? The best-case scenario is that he drags you into his insane world.

"Dillon, I've spent my entire life planning my escape from that place. You could end up majorly regretting being with Remy." Hil picked up an urn and held it between us. "Or worse," he said with sadness in his eyes.

Looking down at the glorified jar, a shiver ran down my spine. But even with what Hil said, I couldn't shake my belief in Remy.

"Hil, if something were ever to happen between me and Remy, he would protect me just like he protects you. Didn't you say that's what he does? Do you think he could stop protecting people if he tried?"

Again finding Hil's eyes I saw his frustration. As we returned to browsing, I thought the conversation was over.

"Do you even know if Remy's into guys?" Hil suddenly blurted out louder than any one should in an urn store.

Instead of answering, I thought about all of the stolen glances and lingering touches that had fueled my fantasies over the years.

"There have been moments when it's just been the two of us that have made me think he could be," I said honestly.

Hil raised an eyebrow. "Wait, when have you two ever been alone together?"

"It's not been often," I admitted, "but it's happened over the years. And sometimes when it does, he looks at me in a way that can't be straight."

Hil still seemed skeptical, but before he could say anything more, he spotted an urn that drew his attention.

"This one," he said holding up one that screamed stately elegance. "What do you think?"

"It's beautiful. I think your father would like it," I said sincerely.

"I'll get it," he said confidently. "And Dillon, please forget about Remy. I know how he looks and how charming he can be but I promise you, it comes at a cost. I couldn't take it if I lost you too."

Looking at him I saw the pain in his eyes. Pulling him into my arms I said, "I love you, Hil. I'll always be here for you. No matter what."

"I couldn't take losing you," he repeated hugging me back.

But holding my best friend in my arms, I came to a decision. As much as I loved HIl, I couldn't ignore how I felt about Remy. I had to at least find out how Remy felt about me.

If he wasn't into guys, then fine. I would accept it and move on. But if there was a chance he felt the same, I had to take it.

A few months ago Hil took a risk by disappearing on everyone who loved him. That risk led to him finding the guy he'll spend the rest of his life with. If Remy was that for me, I had to know. And I was going to find it out after the funeral.

Chapter 4

Remy

Glancing around the tastefully decorated conference room of the building I grew up in, I took in the soft lighting and elegant flower arrangements adorning the tables. The mood was heavy with a mix of grief and nostalgia, but it still felt like the celebration of life that it was supposed to be.

Surveying the guests, I spotted my drugged yet surprisingly sociable mother. She had been handling this better than expected. The miracles of modern pharmaceuticals, am I right?

Past her was my brother, Hil, and his boyfriend, Cali. Seeing Cali always brought a smile to my face. The hulking, college football player who had the balls to openly date a guy, was amazingly easy to fluster. That made teasing him so fun.

'Let's see, what was I going to call him today?' I wondered, walking over to them. Hillbilly? No, I called him that the last time. Redneck? Overused. Tractor-chaser? Mudflap-magnet? Flannel-fucker?

Approaching my grieving brother, I clutched his shoulder and squeezed.

"You did a great job with the wake, Hil. You really did. Everyone's impressed. Dad would have loved it."

Before Hil could respond, I turned to Cali. "And in this situation, a great job means that he didn't put a single picture of cousins kissing anywhere in the place. I know that's weird for you."

"Remy!" Hil protested.

"What?" I asked innocently. "I was ensuring that your Redneck Prince here could follow the conversation. I was being inclusive."

Cali stuttered, wanting to respond but knowing he couldn't out of respect for the occasion. The tortured look in his eyes brought me endless joy.

"Remy, that's not funny," Hil snapped.

I feigned being hurt. "Hil, you're gonna yell at me today? Here? We're at our father's wake. Hil, I'm grieving," I said hoping my smirk wasn't lingering.

Hil, at a loss for words, quieted long enough for me to look over his shoulder. Behind him, standing by himself, was Dillon. He had been watching us. When our eyes met, I felt a vice around my heart.

As he lifted his glass to his lips, he looked away. But it was too late. I was hooked. And for the first time since we had met, I was free to get what I wanted, which was, more of him.

"Remy, all I'm saying is…"

"…that you have no empathy for my grief. Yeah, yeah, yeah. I know, but could we pick this up a little later? I have heartbroken guests I need to attend to," I told my little brother, feeling rejuvenated.

Crossing the room to the man I had wanted for so long, I realized that this was it. I was going to tell him how I felt. I knew I should have been nervous, but I wasn't. The life I had dreamed of and had planned for for years was within my sights. I couldn't wait for it to begin.

Approaching Dillon, I couldn't help but smile.

"Thank you for being here," I said genuinely.

"Of course," Dillon replied, his brown eyes soft and sincere. "If there's anything I can do to help, just let me know."

My mind teetered on the edge of inappropriate thoughts, but I reined myself in. "Actually, there's something I need to discuss with you."

Dillon looked amused. "That's funny because there's something I need to discuss with you. But you should go first."

"Really?" I asked surprised. "In that case, please take the floor," I insisted politely.

"No, go first. Mine can wait."

"No, no. I think you should go first," I said showing him the type of boyfriend I would be to him.

"Remy, please," he said touching my forearm.

Heat washed through me. There was no way I could resist his request now.

"You know what? You're right. What I have to say might influence what you have to say, so I should go first."

"Oh!" Dillon said taken aback. "Okay," he agreed nervously.

I straightened up, seriousness washing over my face. "I've been thinking about you… about us. And… I don't know."

With his tan complexion turning bright red, he put his delicate fingers on my chest. "Wait, before you do, I need to tell you this."

"No, really, I should tell you this first."

Dillon insisted, "Don't say it until I say what I have to say."

"Oh, shit!"

"It's not bad. I promise," Dillon assured me before noticing that I was looking at something behind him. "What's wrong?"

"I'll be back in a minute and I promise you we'll continue this conversation," I said, reluctantly tearing myself away from him.

Crossing the room, I headed toward Armand Clément, my father's greatest rival and the man with whom I had made my deal. In exchange for my release from the mafia world, I agreed to give him my father's illegal businesses.

For it, I would keep the businesses I had created from scratch. On top of that, his organization would offer my family its protection. I had considered it a win-win. He got what he and my father had shed blood over, and I would be free to have what I had built… and Dillon.

Hil, my mother, and I would owe him nothing else. We would never have to see him again.

Yet, here he was flanked by two of his henchmen and a stunning blonde who was young enough to be his daughter. Fighting back my urge to strangle the life out of him, I approached him standing close enough to smell his breath.

"What are you doing here, Armand?" I asked not giving him an inch.

"Remy, I'm here to pay my respects," he replied with a hint of sarcasm.

"Bullshit. If you wanted to show your respect you wouldn't have stepped foot onto my father's territory."

"But this isn't your father's territory anymore. It's mine. It's all mine. Thanks to you."

"And our deal was that you would back off and let us live our lives."

"No," Armand corrected with a smirk. "Our deal was that I would treat you like family. So, I'm here… for family."

I stared at his smug face wanting to bury my fist into it. I couldn't, though. Not here. Not now.

"Cut the crap and get to the point, Armand. Why are you here?"

The scar-faced man with a body built on indulgence, released a snake of a smile.

"That's why I like you. You always get right to business. Okay, here it is. I've been doing some research. It turns out that the businesses I allowed you to keep are worth a bit more than I would have guessed. My accounts say more than a billion."

"You mean the businesses I built from scratch without my father's help."

"No, I mean the ones that you built on the back of your father's empire—an empire that is now mine."

"That's not the way it worked. My father had nothing to do with my companies."

"But his money did. Money that came out of the blood of my people, at my expense."

I clenched my fists, struggling to keep my cool. "Armand, I gave you everything else. What more do you want?" I demanded.

His eyes glinted with mischief. "Actually, what I want is to make you a generous offer. I won't ask you for the share of your businesses that many would say I deserve. Instead, I'll give you a way to ensure that no harm will ever come to anyone you love."

"And how's that?"

"By uniting our families." He gestured to the young woman standing beside him. "I want you to marry my daughter, Eris."

I stared at him stunned, then laughed. "You've gotta be kidding."

Armand's face hardened. "This is not a joke, Remy. Marry my daughter and our families will be connected by more than just business. I don't offer this deal lightly. Refuse and I will take it as a great insult."

My gaze traveled from Armand to the beautiful woman beside him, then to Dillon, who was watching intently from across the room. I knew what Armand was suggesting, but it didn't matter. I couldn't do it. I wouldn't.

"Look, I appreciate the… offer, but I can't marry your daughter."

His eyes narrowed. "I suggest you reconsider, Remy. You don't want to insult me. Not about this. If you did, there will be… consequences."

Hearing his threat, my heart raced. Quickly weighing my options, I looked around the room again. I was in an impossible position. I couldn't risk the safety of my family, nor could I put Dillon in danger. But marrying Eris would mean giving up any chance I had with Dillon, the man I loved.

How could I do this? I couldn't do it. But how could I not do it?

Armand's meaty hands clutched my bicep pulling me aside and snapping me back to reality. I was about to tell him to go to hell and face the consequences when he lowered his voice speaking from one man to another.

"I can see that you're torn. Maybe there's someone else you would prefer to be with?"

"Get to your point," I insisted not about to discuss my feelings for another guy with him.

"My point is that we are men. And men like us can't be contained. I wouldn't expect you to be. All I would expect from you is a wedding and an heir. Past that, who is to say what you do? Live your life without insult to me and I wouldn't care what you get into."

I stared at Armand stunned. Was he proposing that I cheat on his daughter?

"In my family, it's a tradition," he confirmed making me hate him more.

My mind raced fueled by anger and helplessness. I again considered refusing when I looked at his henchman and the barrel-shaped man pulled back his jacket revealing the butt of his gun. Armand had come ready for bloodshed. I couldn't let that happen in a room full of people I cared about… and Cali.

With my thoughts racing towards panic, I gritted my teeth and said, "All right!" It came out before I knew what I was saying.

"What was that?"

My jaw clenched after taking a moment to consider the situation. He had me.

"I'll marry your daughter," I told him stunned by the words coming out of my mouth.

Armand's smug smile returned. Quickly walking away from me, he addressed the room commanding everyone's attention.

"Ladies and gentlemen, I have great respect for the man we are here to honor today. We might have had our differences but the time for disagreements is over.

"To that end, I would like to announce happy news on an otherwise sad day. It is the engagement of my daughter, Eris, to Remy Lyon, a union that will allow peace and prosperity to flourish for all. Let our once bitter rivalry end here and let our great families now become one.

"Let's hear it for the new couple," he demanded smiling from ear to ear.

Polite, confused applause filled the room. Disbelief was etched on my family's faces. It was surreal. What had I done? The reality of my decision didn't hit me until a shocked Dillon caught my eye. His disappointment and hurt were inescapable.

The tingling excitement I'd felt about talking to him was gone. Replacing it was a hollow, aching emptiness. I'd given up my chance at love. And for what?

But staring at him, I realized that after coming so close to having him, I couldn't just let him go. Even if I couldn't be with him, I had to have him near me. I knew I had to offer him something.

"Dillon," I called out, as he headed for the back door looking like he was about to cry. He stopped. Catching up to him, I wrapped my hand around his bicep. He was so small. Pulling him close, he refused to look at me.

"Is that what you were gonna tell me? That you were gonna marry that woman?" he spat mired in jealousy.

"No. It wasn't that at all."

"So you just weren't gonna say anything about it?" he said finally looking me in the eyes.

"That's not what I meant."

"What then?"

He had a point. What was I going to tell him? Should I tell him that I had just sold my soul for the life of everyone in here? It was the truth. But not even I had such a martyr complex.

No, I had had other options and I had made my choice. Now I had to live with it. But that didn't mean I would let Dillon go. According to Armand, I didn't even have to. Though, my proposal for him to be my boyfriend probably had to change.

"Would you consider working for me? I could use someone I trust in my businesses."

He hesitated, his gaze locked on mine. Caught off guard, he looked confused.

"Remy, you know I'm still in college, right? I've got at least a year left before I graduate."

"But, it's about to be summer break, isn't it? And when you graduate, you're gonna need work experience. So, to that end, I would like to hire you as my…"

"…your secretary?" Dillon interjected.

I looked at him surprised by his modest assumption. I had come up with the idea on the fly so I didn't actually know what I was going to propose. But it helped to know his expectations.

"No," I retorted. "My assistant. You'll help me on a daily basis and I'll have access to you whenever I need you."

"Sounds like a secretary to me," Dillon persisted.

I shook my head, "It's not."

"Would I be sitting at a desk outside your office?"

The thought of being able to look up at any time and see him instantly made my cock hard. "Absolutely. That part is non-negotiable."

"That's a secretary," he concluded still not hinting how he felt about the idea.

"Call it what you will. The only thing that matters to me is, do you accept?"

Chapter 5

Dillon

I sat in the chic Soho coffee shop, rubbing my sweating palms against my jeans, waiting for Hil. My heart raced, wondering what he'd say about me accepting Remy's job offer. He'd been right about Remy not leaving the Mafia world behind. And now I was willingly entering it.

The coffee shop was a blend of modern and vintage, with exposed brick walls, sleek leather seating, and a warm, inviting atmosphere. It was a place we had frequented as kids. So many of our summer afternoons were spent here sipping coffee, imaging ourselves more grown up than we were with Hil's bodyguard a booth away.

I saw the same memory in Hil's eyes when he entered. Giving him a nervous smile when his gaze settled on me, he made his way over.

"I chose this place because I thought it'd bring back a few memories," I told him as he sat down.

Hil looked around, taking in the familiar surroundings.

"If it weren't for you, I would know nothing about New York," he admitted. "We used to come here pretending to be adults. Now I'm living with my boyfriend and you're a year away from graduating college. It's weird."

"Yeah. Weird," I said with a chuckle, the nostalgia warming me despite my anxiety.

Taking a deep breath, I soaked in the last of our old dynamic and said, "Hil, Remy offered me a job."

His expression remained unreadable. "You shouldn't take it, Dillon," he said firmly.

My eyes welled up. Looking at my lap, I muttered, "Okay."

A tear slipped down my cheek, and Hil's hand reached out to comfort me.

"Why are you crying?" he asked softly.

I sniffled, meeting his gaze. "Why do you think I'm not good enough for your family?"

Hil sighed, his eyes filling with concern.

"That's not it at all, Dillon. That's not it at all. My whole life, I've felt trapped in my family's crazy life. I don't want you to join me in this cell." He paused, reminiscing. "You don't know what it was like growing up in that penthouse cage, where the only friend I had befriended me out of pity."

I shook my head, denying his claim. "That's not why we're friends, Hil. We're friends because I love you." My voice trembled as I continued, "And I'm really tired of being your family's charity case. I'm grateful for it. Don't think I'm not. But I want to stand on my own.

"If I accepted Remy's offer, maybe I could do that. And maybe if I earned my way, I could take you out instead of always depending on your generosity."

Having heard what I said, Hil wiped his eyes, sniffling.

"I don't want you to get involved with Remy, Dillon. And it's not because you're not good enough for our family. I already think of you as a brother."

"Then, I don't understand. Why don't you want us together?"

"It's because I need you, Dillon. And I know if you got involved with him, he'll do something that will get you hurt. Once that happens, you'll realize you're too good for people like us, and then… you won't want to be friends with me anymore," he admitted as his tears continued to flow.

"I know it's selfish, but I couldn't stand to be alone again, Dillon," Hil added, his voice cracking. "And you're all I have. I don't want to lose you."

I reached out and squeezed his hand. "Hil, nothing will ever break up our friendship. And you'll never be alone again. Not only do you have Cali but I'm not going anywhere. I promise."

Hil smiled through his tears, nodding. "I'm so lucky to have you both. But please, promise me you won't get involved with Remy. I'll do anything. If you need more money, I can get the scholarship committee to increase your stipend."

I shook my head. "I don't want that, Hil. I want to start earning my own money. And I want to take Remy's job offer with your blessing."

Hil hesitated for a moment, then finally gave in. "Alright, Dillon. You have my blessing. But promise me one thing – don't fall for my brother's charms."

I smiled. "I promise."

"Thank you," he said leaning in and hugging me.

Holding him, I looked around at the place we had once pretended to be adults and wondered if I had made a promise I could keep.

A week after accepting Remy's job offer, I walked into his stylish Brooklyn brownstone for my first day. I didn't know what to expect but when Remy stepped out of his office to greet me, my thin suit pants couldn't hide my excitement.

Remy's 6'2″ muscular frame filled out a crisp white shirt like it had been painted onto him. And with his sleeves rolled up, his forearm tattoos were on full display. I could barely speak, feeling a wave of desire wash over me. It was like I was 14 again, uncontrollable boners and all.

"Dillon, I'm so excited to finally have you…"

"… here?" I stuttered.

"Where ever you'd like," he replied with a smile and enough suggestion to drop me to my knees. "Now, the first item on our agenda, come with me," he said quickly changing to a serious tone.

"Where are we going?" I asked, my voice sounding weak as I barely had time to set down my belongings.

"We're doing a walking meeting. That sounds professional, right? Yes, we're doing a professional walking meeting," he said, leading me back outside.

"Will I need to take notes?" I replied reaching for my phone and some semblance of professionalism.

As I pulled it out and navigated to my notes app, he looked at my ancient device and sighed.

"Nope. That will not do. The first thing on your agenda, get yourself a new phone. We'll call it a company phone, but it's yours. Get whichever one you'd like," he said assertively.

"Okay," I replied, surprised by his generosity.

"The next thing on our agenda, there's a Japanese crepe shop nearby that I've been dying for you to try," Remy declared.

"For me to try?" I asked, trying to keep my composure despite barely being able to see straight.

"Yeah. I had it in Japan, then again in Taipei. When I discovered a shop just down the street, I thought, 'you know who would love this? Dillon. Dillon would definitely love this.' Now here you are."

"You were sure that I would love it?" I asked, overwhelmed by his crackling charm.

"And here you are," he repeated.

"And here I am," I confirmed, trying to concentrate on anything but the way Remy's shirt clung to his muscles.

Approaching the shop, I noticed a huge line snaking outside the door. Remy smirked, pulling out his phone.

"They have an app?" I observed, raising an eyebrow.

"They didn't," Remy confessed. "But then I tried one of their crepes, purchased the company, and then built them an app."

I chuckled. "Yet there's still a line."

"The app's still in beta. I wanted to give it rigorous testing before we released it to the public," he explained devilishly.

"So this is your personal app to get Japanese crepes whenever you want?" I asked, my heart pounding from the intensity of his gaze.

Remy smirked. "You've gotta watch them make it. It's very cool."

As we watched the crepe batter being smoothed and flipped on a circular hot plate, I was fascinated. With it cooked, sliced bananas were placed on it and rolled.

Filling it with ice cream and topping it with whipped cream, it was torched into a crème brûlée. It looked amazing! But nothing could prepare me for my first bite.

"Oh my god!" I exclaimed, my eyes fighting to leave my skull.

"Right? Best million I've ever spent," Remy said with a satisfied grin.

I coughed, hearing the price. But then took another bite.

"Yeah, probably," I agreed digging in.

Sitting at a two-top opposite the guy I had been in love with my whole life and eating the most incredible desert I've ever had, I was in heaven. I never wanted this moment to end. When it did and I was left dipping in and out of the pools in his eyes, I brought up the obvious.

"So, I'm here. You have me. You can do with me whatever you want. What's my job going to be? And if you say Japanese Crepe app tester, know that I will test the crème brûlée out of that thing."

Remy laughed. "If that's your dream, have at it. Personally, as long as you show up every day looking gorgeous, I don't care what you do. And, by the way, you're doing an excellent job so far."

I playfully rolled my eyes hiding that my suit pants had lost another round to my erection. But eventually, when I was again able to stand, we got up and walked back to the office.

"So, what does your business actually do?" I asked as the blood slowly returned to my brain.

"During the last downturn in the economy, a lot of companies were cash-strapped. I provided the capital for them to meet their expenses in exchange for a stake in the company and generous interest rates."

"Wait, are you a loan shark?" I blurted out.

Remy burst into laughter. "When you're rich, it's called being a Series D investor."

We approached the brownstone's office door and entered. "Does the 'D' stand for dick? Because that's what loan sharks are," I quipped.

"Officially, it doesn't. But let's be real. Sometimes a little dick is what some people are looking for," Remy replied, smirking.

I blushed. "I wouldn't know anything about that."

"You're more familiar with the bigger dicks? I would never have guessed that about you. But rest assured, Mr. Harris, my firm can help."

Knowing I was turning bright red, I subtly brushed the front of my pants wondering how much was showing. But hearing someone clear their throat, we both looked up. Seeing who stood in front of us, I froze in panic.

Chapter 6

Remy

Seeing Eris Clément in the waiting area of my office ripped me out of the fantasy that I had briefly allowed myself and threw me back into reality. Armand's pampered princess sat posed on my Le Corbusier chaise with her perfectly sculpted blonde curls and icy blue eyes that made clear her disdain for anything that got in her way.

Instinctually, I turned to Dillon beside me. He was visibly unnerved. I hated how she affected him.

"What are you doing here?" I asked, annoyed.

Eris offered a coy smile. "Can't a girl just visit her soon-to-be husband at work?" she asked making the hairs on my arm stand on end. As I gritted my teeth she added, "I brought you an engagement gift, Silly."

"What?" I asked, thrown off by her gesture. What was she doing?

"Things between us may not have started the way either of us would've chosen, but we can still make the best of it, can't we?" She gestured toward a small box on the table. "Open it."

I hesitated again looking for Dillon's reaction. He was as confused as I was. Turning back to the pale blue box with the white ribbon, I picked it up and stared at it."

"It's not a bomb, Remy. I'm sitting here with you," she said sarcastically.

Wanting to get this exchange over with, I pulled back the ribbon and lifted the lid. Inside was a watch that took my breath away.

"How did you know I collect watches?" I stammered, looking up at Eris.

"Remy, you're a man of class and taste. Of course, you'd collect watches," she replied with a pleased smile.

Dillon stepped closer, curiosity getting the better of him. "What is it?"

"It's a Richard Mille RM 56-02 Tourbillon Sapphire. It's a very rare watch," I said trying to remember the last time I saw one in person.

Dillon leaned over for a closer look. "You can see straight through it. It's like the parts holding the hands are floating between glass. It's amazing," he admitted.

I looked at him, then back at Eris. "It's two million dollars amazing," I said, struggling to find the right words. "I can't accept this. It's too much."

Eris folded her arms. "I'll be your wife, Remy. Nothing is too much for my future husband."

Seeing Dillon's shaken expression, I got ahold of myself. "Yeah, I've been trying to find one of these," I said casually.

Eris' eyes gleamed as she asked, "Can I put it on you?"

Fighting the urge to refuse her, I relented as she slid the watch onto my wrist. Still overwhelmed by what I was looking at, I said, "Eris, I don't know how to thank you."

"I do," She replied with a sinister smile. "Never take it off."

Jokingly, I responded, "I'm not sure I would want to."

"And fire him," Eris continued, nodding toward Dillon.

"What?" I asked, again caught off guard by her.

"I think you heard me," she said smugly.

"I can't do that," I declared, darting my eyes over to Dillon, who looked shell-shocked.

Eris scoffed. "Why not? Secretaries are a dime a dozen, aren't they? And it's such an easy way to make your future wife happy."

I glared at her feeling a fire that could melt steel. "Dillon isn't my secretary," I said fighting not to explode.

"Oh, really?" Eris asked, her eyes narrowing. "What is he, then—your lover? Because, forced marriage or not, I will not be humiliated like my mother was," she said unraveling. Quickly catching herself, she paused. Straightening her back she added, "I'll have your head on a plate before I let that happen." And then smiled like she had just shared a weakness for chocolate.

I stared back at her stunned. There was no doubt that Eris was Armand's spawn. After letting her threat hang in the air for a moment, she laughed. The woman was nuts. I was sure she was as capable of killing as her father was.

Knowing I had to do something before things got out of control, I took a step between Eris and Dillon.

"As amazing of a meal as that might be, that's not what's happening here."

Eris raised an eyebrow. "No? Then what is?"

I hesitated for only a moment before saying, "I hired Dillon to head a special project, one that he is uniquely qualified for."

Eris looked unconvinced. "Which is?"

Trying to think quickly, I said, "He's here to create a community outreach center."

"He is?" Eris asked suddenly confused.

"I am?" Dillon asked, equally as surprised.

"You are," I affirmed. "I was going to have you do a trial period with the company to ensure that we worked well together before offering it to you, but I guess that ship has sailed."

Eris crossed her arms, still suspicious. "A community outreach center."

I nodded. "Of course. What you don't know is that Dillon is a recipient of our family scholarship. Not just that, he's from the type of community I'm hoping to reach out to. His mother is our housekeeper. Dillon is practically a member of the family."

Eris considered this. "So, he's like your brother?"

"He's my brother's best friend, who our family has cared for since he was 14," I explained.

Eris smirked. "Oh, he's your family's charity case. Well, I get that."

"I wouldn't phrase it like that, but you get the point."

"Of course," Eris said, her tone lightening. "For a minute there, I thought he was going to be a problem with, you know, us."

"Are you kidding? You thought I was into guys?" I asked regretting it as soon as I said it.

Eris relaxed and chuckled. "Yeah, I guess that would have been silly. Men like you aren't into guys," she said slithering to me putting her hands on my chest and her lips close to mine.

I gathered her wrists and eased her away. "But just because I'm not into him doesn't mean I'll ever be into you. Eris, there is no us. I think we should make that clear now. I have agreed to marry you and someday, if necessary, we might have kids. But that's it. There will never be anything more."

Eris looked unconvinced. "It sounds to me like you are issuing a challenge."

"That's not how I would interpret it," I said, narrowing my eyes at her.

"Potayto, potahto," she shrugged casually.

I chuckled despite myself. "Do I need to make myself clearer?"

Eris raised an eyebrow. "Do I? Because in the end, you will be in love with me."

"Eris…"

"Husband," she said cutting me off, her voice dripping with sarcasm. We both smiled knowingly at each other.

"And here I was afraid our marriage would be boring," she said. "Enjoy the gift. And you," she added, pointing at a stunned Dillon, "remember that there's room on that plate."

"Eris!" I exclaimed, immediately brought to a boil.

"I'm kidding," she said, rolling her eyes. "It was nice meeting you, Dillon. Make our family proud."

Before I could say anything else, Eris spun on her heel, her blonde hair swishing as she made her way out. With the door closed behind her, a fist gripped my heart as I considered what Dillon would say.

Chapter 7

Dillon

My heart raced as I tried to process what had just happened. The humiliation I felt from Remy's words and Eris' presence had ripped my chest open. It ate away at my confidence in a way that nothing else could.

Not only had he made me second-guess my place in their glamorous world, but he had laughed off the idea that he could be attracted to me. I had been such a fool to think that someone like Remy could be interested in someone like me. I was just his family's charity case who was now "uniquely qualified" to give Remy what he wanted.

"Is that all I am to you, then?" I said turning to him, my voice breaking. "A charity case? Someone to fill a gap in your perfect little world by being poor and mixed race?"

Remy looked taken aback by my outburst. "Dillon, that's not what I meant—"

"Well, it sure as hell sounded like it!" I shot back, my insecurities roaring to life.

For a moment, Remy remained silent. When he spoke his casual confidence was gone. Good, he deserved to feel like I did.

"Please, help me understand what I said that hurt you," Remy said painfully.

As much as I wanted to be angry at him, his vulnerability quickly extinguished my fire. In all of the years I had known him, I had never seen this side of him before. It made me fall for him more. I hated myself for it.

With melting resistance, I stared into his eyes. Pushing down a lump in my throat, I realized that I was about to tell him something I had never shared with anyone.

"You don't know this about me because I've never said it aloud before, but I know that I'm basically Hil's pet. He was lonely and needed a friend so your family went to the poor people's pound and found me."

"What?" Remy said feigning shock.

"Don't deny it. I know what other people think when they see me with Hil or you. I don't dress like your family does. I don't look like you do. I don't fit in," I admitted, my voice shaking.

"Occasionally, I let myself believe I might truly have a place in your world, that I could be someone you genuinely care about. But every time I come crashing back to reality, feeling like nothing more than a token poor, black friend you all keep around for laughs."

Remy listened, his eyes never leaving mine. When I was done, he didn't know what to say. I didn't think there was anything he could say. I knew I was right.

But when his gaze hit the floor, he found his voice and quiet confidence.

"Dillon, I want to share something with you. It's something my father once told me. He said, "When you embrace your true self, you'll be rewarded.""

I looked at him, a small part of me daring to hope that maybe he wasn't just talking about life philosophies. That maybe he was talking about us.

"Embracing one's self is never easy, and it can be terrifying," Remy continued. "But... perhaps your background and experiences aren't your weaknesses but your strengths. I can assure you that no one in my family has ever seen you like you've described. And I, for one, think there's so much more to you than you give yourself credit for. So to hear how you think of me, and yourself, breaks my heart," he said nearly in tears.

Lost in the words of the man I had been in love with for so long, I brushed against an idea that was tantalizingly just out of reach. My heart pounded at the prospect. Could there be strength in the things I had run from for so long? I didn't think so. But, still, what if?

What would that mean for me? What would that look like?

"I…"

"What?" he asked when I didn't continue.

No, I couldn't do this. "Remy, I…"

Hearing my tone, he cut me off.

"Dillon, look, I can't pretend to know what it was like being you. I'm white. I'm rich. I'm incredibly good-looking," he said drawing my attention to the brief return of his cocky smirk. "My point is that I don't know what it's like to be you, but I'd like to. And, I was sincere about you creating a community outreach center for me and my family.

"I admit that I didn't think of it until I was forced to. I would have been completely content to just have you show up every day so I could look at you," he said with a smile.

"Remy," I began not able to take his flirting now that I knew he didn't have feelings for me.

"Consider it," he said lightly taking my bicep in his large hand. "Think about how much good you could do. Please, just do that. Will you do that?"

I considered his offer for a moment. It wasn't a bad one. And someone like me creating it would be a hell of a lot better than if he or Hil acted like the great white saviors.

"I'll consider it," I told him wondering if I was making a mistake by even doing that.

Remy's smile beamed. "Brilliant. Also, think about where you would put the place. It could help you make your decision."

"You mean, it could help me decide to do the thing you want me to do?" I asked snidely.

"Of course," he replied with equal measure. Letting his smirk fade, he added, "But seriously Dillon, I want you to do what feels right to you. Despite of what you think, I really care about you. I would do anything to make you happy."

'Everything but love me,' I thought. "Okay," I told him before ending my day early and heading home.

As the train back to my apartment in New Jersey rumbled beneath me, the fantasy I had of Remy and me being together felt like a distant dream. I couldn't shake off the sting of what he had said about me to Eris. His laugh at the thought of liking guys echoed in my ears. The weight of it was a cruel reminder that he didn't, couldn't, feel the same way I did.

Leaning my head against the cold glass of the train's window, the scene with Eris replayed in my mind. The two looked like perfect dolls that were designed to be together. Why had I thought Remy had wanted to be with me?

It wasn't hard to recall. I could remember the very moment I imagined having a life with him. It was the day after that embarrassing naked dancing episode at Remy's parents' place that still made me cringe.

When he arrived the second night, he said he was there because he had received an alert from their security system. He told me he had come to make sure I wasn't throwing another unauthorized dance party. It had to have been a joke. But if he hadn't gotten an alert, then why was he there?

"Nope, no party tonight," I had said turning who knows what shade of red.

"That's too bad. I was bored and looking for a show," he said with his way too charming smirk.

"Well, there's none here," I assured him at the time thinking I would never take off my clothes at their place again.

His eyes lingered on me in silence. As self-conscious as I was, I would have melted under his steely gaze if he hadn't quickly asked, "Have you eaten yet?"

The simple question caught me off guard. My heart pounded unexpectedly at the small gesture of thoughtfulness.

"Not yet. You?"

"No. I was thinking of grabbing a slice. Would you be interested in coming?"

I knew that it was meant to be an innocent invitation from my best friend's brother, but I couldn't help myself. My dumb gay ass wanted it to be a date. And it certainly felt like a date.

Remy opened doors for me, paid for everything, and the way his eyes sparkled when he laughed made me weak in the knees. Over pizza, he told me stories about Hil growing up. When I asked him about himself, though, he wasn't as open. Instead, I saw pain flicker in his eyes. It made me fall for him more.

After we finished our pizza, I expected him to say goodbye but he didn't. Instead, we walked in silence towards his parents' place. And, desperately not wanting the night to end, I steadied my trembling young body and asked,

"Do you like ice cream?"

"Do I like ice cream? Hell, yeah!" he replied his face lighting up.

I told him about a place I had heard of just a few blocks away that was supposed to be really good. Excited, he led me there. After trying a few samples, he mentioned another ice cream shop that was rumored to be even better.

"Better than this?" I asked sampling the best ice cream of my life.

"There's only one way to find out," he said beaming.

After trying that place, it felt like we were on a mission to find the best ice cream in New York. Whipping out my phone, I located the highest-rated ice cream shop in the city. He bet me that nothing could be as good as the one we had just tried. So onto the next place we went.

Trying that one and finding that it wasn't as good, I searched a map of the area hoping to extend our adventure.

"I'm sure there's one that's better," I told him scanning reviews trying to decide which it would be.

"Why don't we just try them all?" Remy suggested excitedly.

"All of them?"

"Why not? Do you have somewhere else you need to be?"

"I was just going to catch up on TV tonight."

"Then, what do you say? Do you wanna find out what the best ice cream in New York City is?"

We walked the entire night, laughing, and hopped up out of our minds on sugar. When the last of the shops closed and we ate our final sample, we leaned against the railing staring out at the river. The moonlight twinkled on the rippling water and I wanted him to kiss me.

Silence had fallen over us. My sixteen-year-old body needed his. I shivered yearning for him to hold me. But he never did. Instead, he walked me back. Standing in the doorway of his parent's place with him not coming in, I could have cried I wanted him so badly.

"It's late," I told him. "Why don't you just sleep in your room? …Or wherever," I said welcoming him into my bed.

"I shouldn't," he said, his eyes tormented.

"Why not?" I dared to brush his forearm, hoping to draw him closer.

"Because I don't trust myself," he said with a tortured smile.

"Because he didn't trust himself," I said aloud remembering his words.

What did that mean? For the past four years, I had chosen to believe that it meant he wanted me. That he liked me back.

After replaying it in my mind for months, I declared that he had only said it because of our age gap. He was just being respectful. So the next time I saw him, I tried to tell him that I didn't care about stuff like that. But either he didn't understand, or he didn't want to, because it didn't change anything.

Now, as the pain from every heartbeat threatens to bring me to my knees, I understand that I had gotten the most romantic evening of my life all wrong. Remy had only come that night because of a security alert. And our citywide ice cream tour had only been about his love for the dessert.

Having spent a million dollars on a shop of his own, he obviously really loved the stuff. None of it was ever about him having feelings for me. I had always been nothing more than his family's charity case.

As the city came into view again through the train's window, I considered how many other things about my life I had gotten so wrong. There had to have been a lot. Looking over the sprawling city bathed in the setting sun, I wondered if I was the only person to have ever misinterpreted something so badly. I couldn't be, could I?

Because the only thing special about me was that a rich family saw me as a convenient playmate for their gay son. The only thing that differentiated me from everyone else was luck. My mother was luckily assigned to the Lyon's as their housekeeper. And their gay son was luckily my age and lonely.

It was only those two things that took us from the projects of Brownsville to my mother owning a home and me being a year from graduating from college. As heartbroken as I was, I was still lucky. There were millions of kids like me who would never get what I had gotten.

And wasn't that what Remy's proposal was about, me helping him spread his family's charity to others? That was a good thing, wasn't it? So, as much as it hurt to accept that that was all he saw me as, didn't I have a responsibility to those who weren't so lucky?

For the next few days, I didn't go into the office. Instead, I did what Remy had suggested. Walking the boroughs, I considered a suitable location for his community outreach center.

Eventually, my wandering led me back to the projects in Brownsville. It was where I was born and where Mom and I lived before she got her job with the Lyons.

As I strolled through the area, I ran into a group of guys I hadn't seen since elementary school. They were hanging around in front of the building drinking beers with their shirts off. It was the middle of a weekday. My heart clenched thinking that could have been me if not for a little luck.

Recognizing me, their faces lit up. After friendly greetings and brief small talk, I continued on.

Another of the privileges I received from the Lyons was not having to hide who I was. Considering how little I could hide being gay, I might have been eaten alive if I had stayed here. As a kid, I had heard about guys being beaten to an inch of their lives for flirting with the wrong guy. Remy's family had rescued me from that.

As I continued my walk through the old neighborhood, my senses were overwhelmed by the area's harsh realities. The faded signs, the echoing engines from narrow streets, the smell of full trash bins. It was day and night compared to where I now lived in New Jersey, much less Remy's neighborhood in Brooklyn.

Continuing down Pitkin Avenue, my thoughts flashed back to the challenges Mom had faced raising me single-handedly. I could never stop the anger from boiling up whenever I thought about this. It shouldn't have had to be that way. I shouldn't have had to grow up without a father. And as I thought more about it, I realized exactly where Remy should put his community center.

With the decision made, a wave of anxiety washed over me. Not only was I going to have to tell Remy where and why, but he would expect me to work with him to build it. Thinking about working that closely with him, smelling his manly leather scent every day, made me weak in the knees. It was like a vise gripped around my heart.

But I had to put my feelings aside. This outreach center was more important than whatever I was experiencing. I owed it to kids like me. Living in this harsh environment, they deserved the same opportunities the Lyons gave me. So with a newfound determination, I vowed to fight through my selfish pain and face Remy with my proposal for his center.

The next day, I stormed into Remy's office powered by anxiety and resolve. Determined not to get distracted by feelings, I immediately was. For a moment I had forgotten what he looked like in a crisp white dress shirt with rolled-up sleeves. Did the man have to show off his tattooed forearms like that? No one deserved to be that sexy. It wasn't fair.

Looking up from his large mahogany desk, a bright smile spread across his face.

"Dillon! It's good to see you. Are you here because you've considered my proposal?"

Was that why I was here? That's right, it was. I nodded. "Yeah. Did you drive to work today?"

Remy looked puzzled. "I did. Why?"

"Could you drive us somewhere? There's a place I want to show you."

Remy agreed, curiosity in his eyes. Walking to his expensive black car, I directed him to Pitkin Avenue in Brownsville. As we pulled up in front of an abandoned two-story building with broken windows and weeds snaking up the brick walls, Remy stared at it confused.

"This is the place?" he said looking up at it through the windshield.

A cold sweat layered my hot skin. I forced myself to speak.

"Yes, this building was where my father lived before he died. He lived here with his family."

Remy frowned glancing between the decrepit building and me.

"But I don't understand. Why put an outreach center here instead of an old YMCA or something? Wouldn't somewhere with more space be better?"

I clenched my fists in my lap gathering the courage to continue. Tears flooded my cheeks despite my efforts. Remy's heartbroken gaze was too much to handle. When he reached out to comfort me, I rejected his touch and pulled myself together.

"No, Remy, hear me out." My voice choked forcing me to swallow and regain focus. "I was the product of an affair. My father cheated on his family with my black mother. He never wanted to have me and I always believed that he couldn't accept me because…" I held up my caramel-colored arms. "Because was I too dark."

My voice wavered as a humiliating memory rushed back.

"So often when my father was alive, I would come here and stand across the street staring up into his lit living room windows. Watching as the people he loved went about their night, I would wonder how it was he could treat his real family so well while pretending I didn't exist.

"I even tried to confront him about it once. Waiting for him where I always stood, I saw him walking up and called his name. When he saw me, he practically ran into building and locked the door behind him.

"It wasn't like he didn't know who I was. Everyone knew he was my father. I was born four blocks away. Yet, he wanted nothing to do with me. So, if there's anywhere in the city that needs to be redefined from hurtful to helpful, it's this place."

Remy's fists clenched the steering wheel trying to suppress his boiling anger toward my dead father. His voice was calm but strained when he finally spoke. "Do you want me to burn this place to the ground so you never have to look at it again?"

I shook my head with my eyes pleading. "No! I want this place to give others the support I couldn't get from it."

Remy nodded, seemingly pacified by my words. His aggressive demeanor gave way to determination. "I understand. I'll buy it, and we'll make this place into something better. Have you given more thought to whether you'd like to help me create it?"

As I considered his question, a smile spread across my face. "I have."

Chapter 8

Remy

Lying in bed alone, staring at the ceiling, I couldn't shake Dillon's story from my mind. I kept replaying the anguish and hurt in his voice as he shared his experiences as a kid. It broke my heart.

It also made me think about my own father – a man who had always been there for me and unquestionably loved me. He was the total opposite of who Dillon's father was. Dillon and my experience growing up couldn't be less alike. Yet there was a part of me that could identify with Dillon's pain.

How could I, though? I had everything the world says you need – wealth, power, privilege. I desired for nothing. Dillon had nothing. So to say that I could identify with his pain was beyond laughable; it was offensive. And every time that thought crossed my mind, it was followed by a wave of guilt.

Despite that, there it was, a feeling that I, a hot, rich, white guy who grew up with a loving father and everything I could ever desire, felt as much pain as Dillon, a guy who grew up poor, black, and rejected by his father. It wasn't right, but it felt true. How could it be?

There was an itch in the back of my mind that brought my thoughts back to my father's expectations for my life. Yeah, I know, boohoo, my rich, loving father was demanding. I knew I had no right to compare my pain to Dillon's but...

Rolling over, burying my face in the pillow, I tried to smother my thoughts away. As I did, the image of Dillon's wounded expression haunted me. I was sure I knew his pain. How, though? I was about to shut off my feelings like I had so many times as a kid when something hit me. I had an idea.

Seeing Dillon already in the office when I arrived the next day, my heart raced. Despite our previously painful conversation, I couldn't keep my eyes off his beautiful caramel skin and unruly curls. But swallowing hard, I put my idea into action.

"I want to show you something," I said, barely holding back the torrent of emotions threatening to spill over.

Dillon looked at me with confusion and then nodded. Leaving the office and driving in silence, we headed to a rundown part of town I wouldn't normally have stepped foot in. After parking, we entered a small

Greek grocery store. As we did, a head popped up above the low aisles.

"Leo!" I said approaching a skinny teen who embodied defiance.

"Mr. Lyon," he replied with a mixture of anger and fear.

"Leo, I want to introduce you to someone. This is Dillon. He was the first recipient of my family's scholarship. Dillon, this is Leo. I have suggested to Leo that he might be our scholarship's next recipient. But, he tells me he doesn't need it."

"I don't," Leo said coldly.

"Right," I replied not hiding my annoyance. I turned to Dillon. "You know what I'm offering him. Do you think you can talk some sense into him?"

Dillon's brow furrowed at my request. It was like he was judging me. Yet, without a word he turned to Leo.

"Why don't you think you need it?"

Leo huffed, crossing his arms defensively. "I don't need his help to take care of my family," he said looking away.

Dillon stared at him. "How old are you?"

"17."

"His father died," I added.

Dillon turned to me with a cynical edge. "So, you want me to tell him my sob story about growing up without a father?"

Tensing my jaw at his tone, I calmed myself and replied, "Whatever you think is best."

Dillon thought for a moment before his expression softened. Refocusing on the kid, he said, "It's Leo, right?"

"Yeah," he snapped guardedly.

"Well, Leo, what's your dream?"

Leo spit his answer. "I don't know."

Dillon's gaze held a glimmer of sympathy as he spoke again.

"Growing up, my dream was to go to Paris. I'm not sure why, but I had seen it in movies and I had a friend who went there all the time, so it meant something special to me, ya know. Eating croissants by the river, having dinner on top of the Eiffel Tower… for a kid coming from where I did, being able to do those things meant that the worst of my life might be behind me. What might signal to you that the worst part of your life is over?"

Leo thought for a moment before a spark briefly lit his eyes.

"What is it?" Dillon asked see it too.

"I don't," Leo said again shutting down.

"No, please, Leo, tell me," Dillon asked with his characteristic empathy.

Leo's eyes dipped. "Animals."

"What?" Dillon asked confused.

Leo took a second to gather his thoughts. "I like animals, ya know. And there are a lot of strays around here. If I had a place where they could live, then..." he said with softened eyes.

"Like an animal sanctuary?" Dillon clarified.

"Yeah, one of those. It would be cool, right?" he said with a smile.

"That would be. So, have you ever thought about becoming a veterinary? They have animal sanctuaries and they help them. They keep them healthy."

"I couldn't do that."

"Why not?"

"You have to go to school for that and I gotta take care of my family, ya know."

Dillon allowed a moment for Leo's words to sink in before responding.

"I like your idea. And it's a beautiful dream, Leo," he said sincerely. "I know right now it's hard to see past the struggles you face day after day. How could you even begin to think about the future when every day presents a new challenge?

"But, here's the thing, ignoring the future won't stop it from coming. And when it arrives, you can be in the same place you are now – full of struggle and anger – or things could be easier, brighter. You just have to make the choice."

Dillon took a step closer, his voice growing more determined.

"Remy has given you the option to make your future better. To make your dream of helping animals a reality. Maybe someone like him can't truly understand how tough your life is, but I can, just like I know you can achieve your dream.

"Believe me when I say that the last thing you want to do is look back on this moment and then have to look into your mother's eyes knowing there was something you could have done to make her life easier, and you didn't take it."

As he finished speaking, Dillon's expression took on a more direct quality. "Do you understand what I'm saying, Leo?"

The teen stared at him for a long moment, weighing Dillon's words. Finally, after what felt like forever, he nodded slowly. "Yeah, I understand."

The tension gradually dissipated as Leo walked off to process everything. I couldn't help but smile about the way things had gone. I turned to Dillon unable to hide my excitement.

"That went well, huh? What do you say about heading back to my place for a Japanese crepe? I've learned how to make it and I'm dying to make one for you. You can tell me what you think."

Dillon hesitated but eventually agreed, seemingly lost in thought as we made our way back to my townhouse. Once inside, I wasted no time, setting to work making the crepe mixture. My hands moved with an energetic precision I didn't know I had.

Mixing the batter, I poured it onto a round hotplate I had bought for this purpose. Evening it out with my leveler, I allowed one side to cook before flipping it to the other.

With it done, I retrieved the ice cream, bananas, whipped cream, and chocolate sauce. Assembling them on the crepe and rolling it into a cone, I topped it with sugar and torched it to a caramelized brown. It looked exactly as I had hoped.

"Here you go," I said, trying to sound as casual as possible.

But as I beamed with pride over my culinary creation, Dillon simmered with anger. He stared at my great achievement with eyes as hard as granite and I wasn't sure why.

"You can't see me any other way than as the charity case you've rescued, can you?" Dillon spat, his voice laced with resentment.

"What? No! Of course I can. Why would you say that?" I replied, taken aback by his accusation.

"Because you exploited me," he accused, his eyes pleading for understanding.

My mind raced through our recent interactions. "When? How?"

"Back there. You used what I told you to get what you wanted," Dillon clarified, the pain evident in his voice.

"That's not what happened."

"Really? Did you ever consider that my history wasn't yours to use as you see fit?" he pressed.

"I…" I stammered, taken aback by Dillon's accusation.

"I didn't think so," he said, his emotions bubbling just below the surface. "You can't see me. All you can see is the pathetic boy who no one loves."

"That's not true. I don't understand where this is coming from," I argued, my heart aching from the pain of his words.

"Remy, you can't exploit my pain," Dillon demanded, his voice wavering.

"I wasn't. That is so far from what I was trying to do," I said defensively.

"Yeah?" he asked doubtfully.

"Yeah. Don't you get it? It's because of my father that his father is dead. His father worked for mine. My father got him killed. Every night I lay in bed thinking about Leo and all of the things my father has done. It suffocates me.

"My entire life is built on the pain of others. It blinds me. I need help. I was asking you to help me, Dillon. Can't you see that?" I said with tears rolling down my cheeks. "I just wanted you to help me."

My heartfelt plea hit Dillon hard. The anger melted from his expression. Wordlessly, he wrapped his arms around me and held me until his eyes glistened with tears.

"I just wanted you to help me," I repeated, my voice choked with emotion.

"I will," Dillon whispered in my ear. "You can count on me."

I slowly pulled away from Dillon's embrace, my cheeks wet with tears. I felt vulnerable and exposed like never before.

"I'm sorry," I muttered, embarrassed by my show of emotion.

No longer able to look at him, I tried to look away. Before I could, Dillon held my chin drawing my gaze back to his. Our eyes locked, and I found myself drowning in his pure, unwavering compassion.

As we stood there, the intensity of our connection, and the lingering air of vulnerability between us, built. Gone were my defenses and sarcasm. In its place was an uncontrollable longing for him.

Dillon's thumb gently brushed along the tear-stained trail on my cheek, sending shivers down my spine. Unable to resist the emotional pull any longer, we both leaned in, our lips drawing closer.

It was a knock on the door that shattered our fragile moment. Pulling us back from the precipice of a passionate embrace, our intimate connection evaporated as someone knocked on the door again.

"I should get that," I said when it became clear that whoever it was wasn't going to leave.

"Probably," Dillon agreed as shaken by our almost-kiss as I was.

Gathering myself, I entered the living room and crossed to the door. I was ready to rip off the head of whoever it was when I opened it and found,

"Eris, what are you doing here?"

"I've been trying to reach you for days. You haven't been returning my texts or calls. I even went to your office, but you weren't there," she replied while pushing her way inside.

"Why are you here?" I questioned with alternating concern and irritation.

She opened her mouth to answer when Dillon stepped past the kitchen door. Spotting him, she froze staring at him with venom. But, as quickly as it happened, she brushed it aside and cheerfully said,

"We have a wedding to plan. There's no way I'm going to do this on my own."

My heart sank at the reminder of the tangled mess our lives had become.

"I can't take part in that right now," I replied, my voice strained.

Undeterred, Eris turned her attention back to Dillon.

"Would you mind getting me a drink, Dear?" she asked condescendingly.

Dillon stalled, asking, "What type?"

Eris sighed, feigning disinterest. "I don't care. Champagne if you have it." Then, with a forced laugh, she added, "It's five o'clock somewhere."

As Dillon disappeared into the kitchen, I braced myself for whatever tirade Eris was about to unleash. As I watched, the confident, casual smile she wore vanished. Replacing it was a deadly-serious glare.

"Remy, allow me to be clear. If you don't start acting like the man I deserve, my father might begin to think you aren't living up to his deal. And who do you think he would blame for that?" she asked before bouncing her eyes toward the kitchen.

"Are you threatening someone?" I demanded, my blood boiling ready to explode.

Eris, unfazed, stepped closer.

"Remy, ask yourself this about me, am I here because I want to be? Do you think my life's goal was to force some mafia prince into a marriage that neither of us wants to be in? Do you think this is the life I dreamed about as a little girl?" she asked sarcastically.

"It isn't. And now I'm fighting for the life I want, just like you are. The only difference is that behind me is a mad man who will burn the world down to get what he wants. Your mad man is dead. So, unless you get with the program and meet me halfway on this, blood will rain down. Not mine. Not yours. But everyone you care about.

"Do you want that? From the way you're staring at me, I'm going to assume you don't. So, stop putting everyone you care about at risk, and help me plan our wedding," she continued with eerie calmness.

"There are millions of arranged marriages that end happily ever after. Help me make ours one of them... so your friend back there doesn't have to die."

As Dillon returned from the kitchen with Eris's drink, he noticed that my demeanor had completely changed. It was as if a shadow had come over me, the weight of Eris's words suffocating my spirit.

I looked at Dillon knowing what Eris had said was true. The men who crossed our fathers ended up dead. Like mine, her father was a hurricane, a force of nature that couldn't be stopped, only weathered.

I needed to protect Dillon from that storm. I was willing to do anything for it. So, erasing any trace of the affection I felt for him, I stared at him coldly and said, "Dillon, you should leave."

His body melted at my abrupt change. Pain spilled from his eyes. Seeing it destroyed me. But I had to remain detached – I couldn't let Eris know how much he mattered to me. I couldn't give her any more leverage.

"Dillon," I repeated, feeling a sharp sting in my chest as I spoke. "Just go. We can talk later."

As he hesitated, I added, with a steely edge, "Now!"

That was when he lowered his eyes, turned to the door, and left leaving me shattered in pieces.

Chapter 9

Dillon

The sun was setting over Brooklyn as I left Remy's townhouse far behind. Heading towards the train station, my footsteps were weighed down by the crushing ache in my chest. The air was unseasonably crisp for late spring, but the cold did nothing to chill the heat that ripped through me.

Why had I allowed Remy to do this to me again? I had fallen into that same trap, exposing my vulnerable heart to the same person who had torn it to shreds before. What broken part of me kept putting myself in this situation?

Hil had warned me about Remy. He had said that Remy would go back to his mafia world, and he had. Hell, he was marrying into it.

Hil also said that Remy would hurt me. Not only had Hil been right about that, but after Remy had done it the first time, I had turned around and had let him do it again. I was an idiot who deserved everything I got.

There was no wonder my own father ran away from me. Even he could see how much of a mess I was. I didn't deserve anything more.

As stupid as I was, though, I had finally learned my lesson. Never again would I give Remy another opportunity to treat me like he had. I got it; the outreach center was important. There were real lives it could affect.

Talking with Leo had shown me that. And being able to make amends meant more to Remy than I could ever have imagined. So I would help him. But that was it. I was done with whatever emotional game Remy was playing.

From this point forward, we were going to be colleagues. Nothing more. If he thought he could hurt me and get away with it, he was about to learn that I could hurt him right back.

I refused to need him. At least not anymore. I was done. I really was. And as the finality of it slowly sank in, tears rolled down my cheeks.

Boarding the same train on which I had decided to work with Remy, I ended my foolish childhood fantasy. Remy and I weren't made to be together. We weren't even destined to be friends.

I was fated to be alone. I always had been. And as the glow of burnt oranges receded behind the towering downtown buildings, I sank into the seat of the train and cried.

The following morning, I woke up with a renewed sense of determination. I had spent all night mentally preparing myself to face Remy, to show him that I could be just as cold and detached as he had been the day before. As I showered and dressed, my resolve strengthened. I began looking forward to the confrontation.

Arriving at work, I strode in ready for the day with my head held high. Surprisingly, Remy's office door was closed. The room lay still and silent. There was no sign of him anywhere.

I shook off my disappointment and focused on the tasks at hand. Busying myself with watering the plants and dusting the shelves, I checked the clock every few minutes. Surely Remy would arrive soon, and then I could put my plan into action.

But as the hours ticked by, the gnawing fear in my gut grew larger. Could Remy be avoiding me just like my father had done all those years ago? A thunder-clap of pain shot through my chest. It hurt more than when Remy had asked me to leave.

Slowly, the cold exterior I had been practicing crumbled. My once steadfast resolve now seemed foolish and hollow. I was simply incapable of hurting Remy like he hurt me.

With the void growing inside me I could no longer focus. When the afternoon slipped away without a sign of Remy, the emptiness consumed me. I was drowning in it.

Over the next two days, Remy remained absent from the office. My heart beat a little faster every time the door rattled, but each time it wasn't him. I remained alone with nothing to do but stare at his vacant office. It was torture.

The image of Remy's empty desk plagued me even as I lay in bed trying to fall asleep. The hurt was like a physical weight on my chest, an all-consuming ache impossible to escape.

I had been ready to give him everything I had, but he didn't want it. I had fooled myself into believing that his engagement wasn't real, but it was. And after making me believe that I was special to him, he left me. Now he wasn't coming back.

This was not the way you treated someone you loved. So that left one conclusion. The man I had been in love with since I was 14 years old, didn't love me. And why would he when no one did?

I returned to work each day after that expecting him not to show yet being hurt all over again when he wasn't there. No one was. It took two weeks before the rattling door was anyone other than housekeeping. So the day when a stumpy, formally dressed man ascended the stairs, I stood and greeted him confused.

"Can I help you?" I asked wondering if he was at the wrong address.

"My name is Robert Wendel. I'm Mr. Lyon's attorney," he said overflowing with anxiety.

"Mr. Lyon isn't here," I informed him.

"Yes. I have papers for you to sign."

"Me?"

"You are Dillon Harris, correct?"

"Yes."

"Then they're for you."

Staring at the lawyer, I thought back to when my mother first started working at the Lyon's. There was a man like this who had shown up at our door. He made it very clear that we were never to talk about anything my mother overheard or saw at the Lyon's residence. The papers she signed were for a non-disclosure agreement, but the threat to our lives if we talked about what we saw didn't have to be written down.

"Oh," I said realizing the extent to which Remy didn't trust me.

Without asking any questions, I quickly signed my name wherever the lawyer directed me to. Each time, my heart clenched a little more. When the last page was signed, he handed me a large manila envelope.

"This is yours."

"What is it," I asked suspecting it was my copy of the paperwork.

"It's the deed to the building for the outreach center."

I froze. "I'm sorry, what is it?"

"The building's deed," he repeated this time searching my face to see if I understood. I didn't. "What you signed was the paperwork for a trust that owned the building. You now have a controlling 51% interest in it."

My mind spiraled. "I'm sorry, I'm confused. What does that mean?"

"It means that, for the most part, the building is yours. A part of the arrangement is that the building's taxes will be paid by the Lyon family for the next 10 years. So you don't have to worry about that. And you can do with it whatever you'd like. Which is, I assume, to create the outreach center you proposed to Mr. Lyon, correct?"

"Correct," I confirmed still unsure of what was going on. Had Remy done this for tax purposes? Was this shady mafia world stuff? "So, I can do anything I want with it?"

"Anything."

"If I wanted to sell it?"

"You could."

"And just so I'm aware, how much is it worth?"

"I can't tell you off the top of my head. But I included the property's appraisal in your package," he said gesturing to my envelope.

I looked down at what was in my hand as if it contained a snake ready to bite. My heart raced thinking about what was inside. Opening it slowly, I reached in and pulled it out. Flipping through the pages, I found one with numbers on it. The appraisal wasn't hard to find. It said that the building Remy had just given me was worth $1.5 million.

"Ahh," I exhaled unable to breathe.

"Mr. Lyon also instructed me to give you this," his lawyer said barely drawing my attention.

He was holding a business card. "He told me that you have an appointment with this person," the lawyer said cryptically.

"When?" I said almost too stunned to take the card.

"I think he meant now."

Leaving the office, I rushed to the address on the business card unsure of what I'd find. When I arrived, a chic woman introduced herself.

"Hi, I'm Melanie. I'll be your personal shopper. Mr. Lyon asked me to dress you like a representative of the Lyon family," she explained as if trying not to hurt my feelings.

I thought for a moment and then looked down at what I was wearing. Knowing I would need to dress professionally for Remy, I had gone to a discount department store. The clothes I bought there were the right size and had fit as they should.

My clothes had always been one of the things that had made me feel like Hil's pet when we went out. He dressed like the son of a billionaire mafia boss, and I dressed like Waldo. There was no hiding the chasm that existed between us.

"Do you mind?" Melanie asked when she saw me hesitate.

"Not at all," I replied as a lifetime of insecurity lifted from my shoulders.

Getting measured and trying on expensive clothing was a little intimidating at first. After all, most of the suits cost as much as a small car. What if I got it snagged on something? I would be in debt for the rest of my life.

But after a few hours of it, I had to admit that it became fun. A lifetime of insecurities melted away as I stared in the mirror at myself. And walking out with $20,000 worth of designer suits, I couldn't help but feel that Remy was trying to tell me something... But what?

Arriving at the office the next day in a $3,000 outfit, I had to admit, it felt pretty good. I had expected no one else to see it until I switched on my computer and was flooded by calendar notifications.

As the day unfolded, architects, designers, and construction experts paraded through the office. Each one treated me like royalty. It was surreal. Then finally, when I couldn't take it anymore, I asked one why they were acting like they were.

"Mr. Lyon told us he would pay for anything you choose and said it was vital that we make you happy," the architect explained softly. "On that note, we brought you a sampling of pastries from Dominique's. Would you care for one as we discuss the plans for the redesign?"

"Sure," I said, still unable to wrap my head around what was going on.

The building, the clothes, everyone kissing my ass, why was Remy doing this? He had made it clear that he didn't want to be with me. Was this his attempt to show me all of the reasons why? Was it to show that he could do all of this for me while I couldn't do any of this for him? I didn't understand.

The next week passed in a blur of appointments and decisions. Tired and unsure of what Remy's endgame was, I continued making choices for the outreach center as if I owned the place. There seemed to be no end to the people I needed to talk to. And even though my meetings ended promptly at 6 whether we were done with our discussion or not, I still spent the rest of the night at the office looking up all of the words they said that I didn't understand. I was dead to the world as I rode the train home.

All that continued until the day I returned to the office and saw that my first appointment was after work hours. There was something that told me that this was it. When I stepped into wherever it was, I was going to find

Remy. He would be waiting for me, armed with his devilish smirk and as charming as ever.

How would I respond to that? Yeah, the clothes and the building were great. It felt life-changing. But I hadn't asked him for any of it.

All I had ever wanted was for him to love me. To hold me and tell me that he would be there for me. I couldn't give him a pass for all of the things he had done just because he had gotten me a few gifts. I couldn't. And he was going to find that out tonight.

As my day ended, I readied myself to see Remy for the first time in weeks. I hardened my resolve. He wasn't going to like what I had to say. It might actually lead to the end of us. The final end. The one we couldn't come back from.

And, as much as I knew that could be the case, I couldn't deny how good it would feel to see him again. He was a complete asshole for doing what he had to me. But, I missed him. The way he looked at me made me feel seen. Remy had a way of making me feel like the most important person in the world. It was a drug that was hard to quit.

Approaching the address, it turned out to be a posh apartment complex in downtown Brooklyn. Had he invited me to his love nest? Was everything he had bought me his way of seducing me? Was that all I was to him – a hook-up?

Stepping off the elevator into one of the fanciest apartments I had ever seen, I looked around for who I was sure was waiting for me.

"Remy?" I asked an empty room.

Slowly circling the place, awestruck by its beauty, it didn't take me long to spot the driftwood dining table and the note tented on top of it. Facing me was my name. Opening it as I picked it up, I recognized the handwriting.

'Consider this a perk of the job. No more late-night train rides. Enjoy your new place. Remy'

Continuing my tour, I entered the bedroom. The view of the city was breathtaking. Opening the closet, I found a wardrobe full of new clothes. There weren't just suits. There was something for every occasion.

This was it. There wasn't an additional surprise. He wasn't coming. Not tonight. Not ever again. It really was over between us. Realizing that, I stepped onto the balcony, relinquished the last of my hope, and cried.

Sleeping in the world's most comfortable bed was weird. You would think that it would make you fall asleep faster. But who could do that, distracted by thoughts of how comfortable it was?

With a light morning schedule, I decided to sleep in. I was now only a few blocks from work instead of the 55-mile commute from New Jersey. It was like a new world. So too was my attitude on life. In the last few weeks, I had shed a lifetime of tears. I was ready to move on.

For some reason, Remy had given me a building. But not just any building. It was the one my father had lived in with his family. Remy might not have known how to be a proper fantasy boyfriend, but he understood a thing or two about poetic justice.

"Remy gave me a building," I said when it hit me again.

Grabbing something from my fully stocked fridge, I decided to take a detour before work. I was going to check out my new place. Getting off the train, I rounded the corner with the building in sight. Watching the renovators enter and exit, I remembered that I had a controlling interest in it. This was insane.

Like I had so many times as a kid, I stopped across the street and stared at it. I had so many painful memories associated with this place I couldn't count them all. Maybe instead of turning it into an outreach center, I should have sold it. I don't know what I was thinking suggesting it as a place I might have to go to every day.

That reminded me of another thing I had to do: I had to start thinking about hiring people. After all, Remy hadn't asked me to help him because of my managerial skills. It was because I was his little brother's poor, black best friend.

I thought about that for a second. Remy hadn't asked for my help despite who I was. He had asked because of it. In this case, being poor and black was my advantage.

Remy had once said to me that when you embrace your true self, you get rewarded. Could he have been right?

Certainly, he wouldn't have given me any of his gifts if I hadn't been who I am. And, the more choices I had to make for the outreach center's design, the more important my opinion felt. I guess it isn't specifically my opinion. It would be the opinion of anyone who didn't grow up with a silver spoon in their mouth.

Seriously, what were these designers thinking? A paintball center? Yeah, that's exactly what the residents of Brownsville needed, a way to shoot at each other recreationally. Nothing bad could ever come from that.

No, the center was going to be for kids. On the first floor would be quiet rooms where kids could just sit and relax because that's what a true safe space looked like. On the second floor would be tutors and counselors. And on the third floor would be the LGBT resources.

For that, we could have mentors come in and speak. Each night of the week could be support meetings, whether it's for gays, bisexuals, trans folks, or women in abusive relationships.

"Dillon?" someone said, drawing my attention. "Dillon, right?"

"Yes," I said, staring blankly at the young, dark-skinned guy in front of me.

Being away from the neighborhood for as long as I had been, hearing my name made me nervous. My life had changed a hell of a lot since I was 13. For one, I no longer pretended to be straight. That didn't make a difference at my college in New Jersey. But poor black communities weren't exactly the epitome of acceptance.

"It's James. Or, I guess Jimmy. We went to school together," the slightly older guy said.

"Jimmy! Right!" I said energetically.

He smiled.

"You have no idea who I am, do you?"

I chuckled embarrassed. "I'm sorry."

"No. Don't worry about it. We didn't really know each other back then."

"Oh, okay," I said, confused. "But we did go to school together?"

"We definitely did," he said with a smile that hinted at more.

I looked at him again. No, I didn't remember him. But, he was cute, and his smile meant something. Lowering my guard, I loosened up.

"Did we have the same classes or anything?" I said with a flirtatious smile I was hoping he would pick up on.

"No. I was two years ahead. But I do remember you."

"Why was that?"

"Well, one, you were cute. Very cute. Still are," he said, confirming my suspicion. "And two, you were the first guy I ever... dared to flirt with."

"Seriously," I asked, not expecting that.

He blushed. "Yeah, you were always so... I don't know, confident back then. You always seemed to know who you were. I was having thoughts and terrified of who I might be. You just were, and accepted it."

I laughed. "I'm glad it looked like that. But I can assure you that wasn't the case."

"Maybe. But, I gotta say, thinking you were gave me hope, you know? I made a lot of decisions based on the guy I thought you were."

"Wow," I said, no longer flirting with him. "Thank you."

"No, man, thank you," he said appreciatively. "So, what are you up to now? You moved out of the neighborhood, didn't you? It was a few years back."

"Yeah. My mother got a job. We ended up moving closer to it. What about you? You still live around here?"

"No. I went to a community college in Virginia. So I was there for a while."

"Virginia? Why there?"

"It's close to the FBI headquarters. I wanted to take a few specialty programs that allowed for easy enrollment."

I froze. "To the FBI? And did you... enroll, I mean?"

Jimmy smiled proudly. "I did."

"Oh, congratulations. What division?" I asked hesitantly.

He leaned closer and lowered his voice. "Organized crime."

"Oh!" I replied, immediately thinking of Remy. "Nice," I said, trying not to panic.

"Yeah. I figured, what better way to give back to the community than to try to get some of the gangs off the streets? What about you? What are you doing now? Real estate?"

I stared at him nervously. "What made you say that?"

"I noticed you looking at the building. It was like you were casing the joint. If I didn't know you, I'd be worried," he joked.

"Oh," I laughed. "I mean, I guess kind of." I paused to choose my words carefully. "I'm working with the person who's turning the building into a community outreach center."

"Seriously? That's fantastic. You know, if you ever want to talk about anything, like how to make sure the gangs don't bother you here, anything really, you should give me a call," he said flirtatiously before pulling out a card.

I had to shut down any thoughts he had about us quickly. The last thing I needed to do was date someone in the FBI while working for the son of one of the biggest mafia bosses in the city.

"I'll be honest, I'm just recovering from a… I don't know what would you call it, a situationship? So I'm not up for anything in that way. But it might be helpful to touch base about safety strategies for the center."

"Of course. Anything you need. Just let me know. It was, ah, good to see you again, Dillon," he said, making sure his interest was clear.

"You too, Jimmy. I mean, James. I'll let you know," I said, holding up his card as he walked away.

Leaving the neighborhood, I thought about my conversation with Jimmy. It was amazing to think that I could have had such an effect on him. Back then, I constantly felt miserable for being gay and not fitting in. Yet, Jimmy had found the strength to be who he was from watching me.

"How?" I asked aloud, trying to understand it all.

Returning to the office, I added something new to my calendar. I needed to start hiring. The programs I imagined for the center had to be designed, and I had no idea where to begin.

Knowing Remy had access to my calendar, I decided to test him. I blocked off time and labeled it 'Start Hiring Process.' Hitting save, I stared at the screen waiting for a reaction. When nothing happened, I chuckled at my unrealistic expectations and went about my day full of meetings.

After reviewing countless designs, and then looking up all of the new words I had heard, I was done. Walking to my new place, I again thought about my encounter with Jimmy. I couldn't shake the feeling there was something important I'd missed about it. As I prepared dinner from the fancy dips lining my fridge, I replayed our conversation.

It wasn't until I lay in bed, drifting off to sleep, that it finally hit me. Remy had said that embracing your true self brings rewards. And despite my personal struggles, Jimmy had been inspired by my true self.

As the thought washed over me, a smile tugged at my lips. Remy had been right. Embracing your true self brings rewards. Rolling over feeling wiser, I cuddled a pillow and quickly fell asleep.

Walking into the office the next morning I found new meetings scheduled on my calendar. A slew of headhunters, job recruiters, and representatives from job posting websites filled the agenda. How was Remy able to get all of this done in one night? There was no way I could ever allow myself to feel anything for Remy again, but I had to admit that he wasn't all bad.

As the weeks passed, Remy and I fell into a routine of indirect communication. I would enter requests in my calendar, and he would make them happen, usually the next day. I wasn't sure why, but our exchanges were strangely comforting. I was almost starting to believe I could handle everything.

During a lunch with Hil when he had flown into the city to visit his mother, I filled him in on my job and all the perks that came with it.

"Remy says you're doing an amazing job," Hil said proudly.

I might have been. But I couldn't help but think of Remy's perks as some sort of guilt payment.

"Thanks. It's nice to hear," I said humbly.

"No, seriously! What you're doing is so great. Do you even know the effect you're going to have on people? I loved my father. I did. But, he did so much wrong.

"It was like he had no conscience. The stories Remy would tell me…," he said drifting off and fighting back tears. "I'll just say that what you're doing means a lot… to the whole family," Hil concluded with a teary-eyed smile.

Staring at Hil, I realized that what I was doing meant more to his family than I had considered. I was still thinking that it was a rich family's vanity project. But both Remy and Hil had been brought to tears when they talked about their father's legacy.

What could he have done that required a community outreach center as a penance? And how was

I the one who could help them? I was a nobody who came from nothing.

I was everything no one wanted to be. I was too gay for the straight world, too black for the white world, too white for the black world, and my mother was a housekeeper. The fact that I could have that type of impact on a family that had everything didn't make sense.

"You were right, you know," I told Hil changing the topic.

"About what?" he asked wiping his eyes.

"About everything. When I had asked you about taking this job, I had been so sure that Remy was done with the world you all had grown up in, yet, within days, he was engaged to the daughter of your family's rival."

Hil looked away sadly, "Yeah."

"And you said that if I allowed myself to have feelings for him, he would break my heart."

It was my turn to tear up.

"Oh, Dillon!" Hil said quickly taking my hand to comfort me. "I didn't want to be right about that. You're not going to leave me, are you?"

I put a confident smile on my face. "Never. I will never leave you," I said sincerely.

Hil squeezed my hand and smiled. "Let me pay for this so we can check out what you've been working so hard on."

"No, I've already paid for it," I said proudly.

Hil looked concerned. "Dillon, you didn't have to."

"I know. I wanted to. I'm making money now. And if I'm ever going to get over my hangups, I need to be the one doing the treating for a change. Allow me to do this for you."

Hil still looked hesitant.

"Please. I need this."

Hil finally smiled and conceded. "Of course. Thank you," he said looking at me in a new light.

Months later, with the opening of the renovated outreach center a day away, I found myself working late in what used to be Remy's office. Alone and immersed in my thoughts, I was surprised by the sound of the door creaking open.

Rounding the desk, I froze in disbelief. Remy was walking towards me staring into my eyes. I was stunned into silence. With him an arm's length away, a tsunami of emotions crashed over me.

When I could again speak, my words were flat. "I'm mad at you."

"Really? I can't imagine why. Your new station in life agrees with you," Remy retorted, his eyes drifting to my attire.

Blushing slightly, I glanced down at my expensive outfit and then glared back at him. "Do you think I care about this?"

"I do. Yes. At least a little," he admitted.

I wanted to deny it. But deep down I knew he was right.

"Are you expecting me to fall all over you with gratitude for what you've done?" I asked tensely.

"I'm not gonna lie, I was kind of hoping," Remy replied, his charm slowly returning.

I stepped towards him. "Well, I'm not. I'm mad at you."

"Okay, let's hear it. What did I do?"

I frowned. "Don't treat me like my feelings don't matter."

"I'm not doing that. I know they do. And, I'm sorry."

"You left me. You made me think that something was developing between us and then you ghosted me… for months. You broke my heart."

Remy paused as pain washed over him. "I did do that. Would you forgive me if I told you that there was a very good reason?"

"Because you had to plan your wedding?" I spit.

Remy looked away to pull my dagger from his heart. "I guess I did."

"And do you know what makes me even madder?"

Remy, standing inches in front of me now, asked, "What's that?"

"It's how much of a hypocrite you are."

"I'm a hypocrite? I'll have to admit that in the thousands of times I imagined this moment, being called a hypocrite hadn't crossed my mind."

"Well, you are."

"Then enlighten me. How am I also a hypocrite?"

"You're a hypocrite because you make this huge deal about the rewards that come from being your true self and then the moment you get the same choice, you do the opposite."

"You think my withdrawing is me denying my true self?"

"I don't think it. I know it."

"That's interesting because I think my true self is someone who does whatever they have to keep the ones they care about safe. To suffer, to endure, to hurt in order to make sure that nothing happens to the ones I love. Are you saying that's not truly who I am?"

"The ones you love?" I asked vulnerably.

"The one I love," Remy clarified.

I softened at his words but still maintained my resolve, "But you're not heartless."

"Who said I was heartless?"

"You did. In your actions."

"Please enlighten me."

"You think you can live your life with your heart locked away denying everything you need and desire, but you can't. You're gentle and vulnerable. You're kind and wonderful. I know you think you should be, but you're not like your father. That's a good thing. And as a wise man once told me, when you are your true self, you're rewarded."

With that, Remy leaned down. Locking his eyes on mine, he closed them and slowly bridged the space between us. As his warm breath brushed against my cheek, I could smell the faint scent of his cologne, a mixture of sandalwood and citrus that sent shivers down my spine. My heart raced while my lips tingled with anticipation.

As if having waited for a lifetime, our lips met— soft, tender, like the hushed stroke of velvet. It was everything I had dreamed it would be. My eyes fluttered closed as I allowed myself to be in the moment. Every nerve in my body came alive as I kissed him back.

His fingers grazed my cheek before gently threading through my curls and cradling the back of my head. Feeling his touch, my arms wrapped around his neck. When his warm body pressed comfortably against mine, our bodies swayed.

As our kiss deepened, the taste of him lingered on my tongue. He was as sweet as the plumpest cherry and I tingled like mint. With my breath caught in my throat, my chest swelled with emotion. In his embrace, I finally realized what was true – this was where I belonged.

"Wait," I said, pulling away.

"You asked me to be my true self. This is me and I want to kiss you. I've always wanted to kiss you.

Watching you play with Hil when we were kids, I wanted to kiss you. I've never been anyone else."

"I can't be the other woman... or man... or person," I insisted.

"You're not. You're the only person. You've always been that."

"What about Eris?"

"What about her? She's the woman I'm forced to marry to keep everyone around me alive. She's not who I want to be with. She's certainly not who I want to have sex with."

"But you do?"

"Do what? Have sex? With her? It would be like sticking my dick into a bear trap. That ain't gonna happen. That will never happen. She thinks it might. But I'm telling you, it won't."

"What, you're just not gonna have sex ever again?" I asked doubtfully.

"It's been this long," Remy said with a frustrated smirk.

"How long has it been?"

"Since I've had sex?"

"Yeah."

"From the moment I realized that you were the one."

"And when was that?"

Remy thought. "Well, I would say from the moment we met. But officially... do you remember when

Hil got kidnapped and I came to your place looking for him?"

"Yeah."

"From the moment you opened the door and I looked into your eyes. That's when I knew I couldn't deny it anymore. I was yours and I would do whatever I had to to make you mine."

"Oh," I said as heat flushed through me.

Not knowing what to do with myself, I asked, "Are you coming to the Outreach Center's Opening tomorrow?"

"That was my plan."

"Good."

"Would you mind if we did something to celebrate afterward?"

I froze. What did he mean by celebrate? It wasn't that I didn't want him there or to celebrate with him. There was no one I would rather be with. This accomplishment was as much his as it was mine. Even when he had left me, he had been there for me. Now I wanted to be with him.

"Nothing fancy," I conceded.

"No guarantees."

"Everything you said was nice. But, I don't want to give you the impression that I've forgiven you for leaving me like that."

Remy nodded, understanding my hesitancy. "Understood."

"So, nothing fancy?"

Remy smiled. "No guarantees."

Chapter 10

Dillon

Hil and Cali exited the stairway waving enthusiastically to get my attention. I looked up and saw Hil's face beaming, his eyes glistening with unshed tears.

"I was just upstairs in the LGBT center," Hil said, clearly emotional. "You did a fantastic job, Dillon."

"Well, it wasn't just me," I replied, touched by his reaction. "A few people contributed. It's crazy how much work and cooperation is required for something like this."

Then, I added reluctantly, "Remy deserves a lot of the credit, too."

Hil cut me off immediately. "Don't you dare give my brother credit for something he had nothing to do with. Not after the way he treated you."

I relented knowing Hil hadn't received an update on things since last night's kiss. But even without that, I couldn't ignore the role Remy played in making the center a reality.

Not only was it his idea, but I was a 21-year-old kid who didn't know anything about anything. He found the designers, the architects, the recruiters, everyone. And after turning the center's creation into a multiple-choice quiz, he put people beside me who pointed at the right answers.

I would have been lost if it wasn't for him. Actually, that's not true. I wouldn't even have attempted to do it in the first place. I wouldn't have had the confidence or the push to look past my insecurities. Without saying a word to me in months, Remy had changed the direction of my life.

"Speaking of credit hogs," Hil muttered under his breath.

"Shit!" Cali exclaimed seeing him next.

As I turned to look at Remy, desire flooded my body. I hated myself for it, but I had given up trying to fight my feelings for him. No matter what Remy did, I would forgive him. Because despite everything, Remy was a good man, and there was nothing that would stop me from loving him.

"Shit, indeed!" I agreed, but for a very different reason.

I waved Remy over, pulling my emotions into check. As he approached, he greeted us with a smirk. "Brother," he said to Hil, nodding. "Redneck Rambo," he added, addressing Cali.

Cali rolled his eyes, his jaw clenched. "I'm gonna go get a drink. Anyone else want one? No? Good," he said before walking off.

"Why do you always treat him like that? You're such an asshole," Hil snapped before hurrying after his boyfriend.

"Why *do* you always treat him like that? You know he's good to Hil, right?" I asked Remy.

"He's the best man I know. He took a bullet for my brother. I mean, Jesus."

"Then why do say those things to him?"

"Don't you find how perfect he is a little annoying?" Remy replied with a smirk. "I mean, either be a great person or have great hair. Make a choice."

"We know what you chose," I said, brushing his shiny black locks.

"Yes. Thank you!" he said resolutely.

"Dillon," Jimmy said, approaching us.

Remembering who he was and what Remy was, I tensed up. "Oh, Jimmy. I mean, James. This is Remy, the owner of the building and the person financing the outreach center."

Remy's brow furrowed as he looked at me, confused. "I don't own the center. I thought you knew…"

I cut him off. "James and I went to junior high together. He now works at the FBI."

Remy's eyebrows jumped to his perfect hairline. "Really?"

"Which division again?" I asked him.

"Mostly the organized crime branch," he said jovially.

"Really?" Remy asked, turning to me, stunned.

"There's a lot of gang activity in the area," I explained. "The kids who come here need to know that they'll be safe. So, when I heard what James was up to, I asked if he was interested in partnering with us in providing a safe space for the kids. And, lucky for us, he was."

"I grew up around here. I know how much a place like this is needed."

"Here, here!" Remy said, hiding the panic behind his eyes. "So you made him an official partner with the center?"

"Yep," I said, staring into Remy's eyes.

"Excellent! Keep your friends close. Am I right?"

"You are," Jimmy said for the first time, hinting that he knew who Remy was.

Remy tightened his lips, trying to smile. "Where is Cali with that drink?"

"Excuse us," I said following Remy as he walked off.

When we were out of Jimmy's earshot, Remy whispered, "You partnered with the organized crime division of the FBI?"

"Not with the department. With James."

"Right. Because anything he discovers while using this as his base of operations will certainly not leave this room," Remy sniped, genuinely rattled.

"Remy, you wanted a community center somewhere it would help people. This is it. And partnering with someone like Jimmy is a necessary evil. Would you have preferred if instead of him it was a drug dealer from one of the local gangs? Because those were my two options."

Remy calmed himself. "I'm not questioning your decisions, Dillon."

"It certainly sounds like you are."

"I'm not. Believe me, I think you did an amazing job. This place would never have existed without your hard work and everything you've done. Thank you, Dillon. You're incredible."

Allowing his compliment to sink in, a smile beamed up from the deepest part of me.

"I appreciate you saying that." I looked into his beautiful, grateful eyes. "And I recognize how hard you worked on this, too. No one else sees it, but I do."

Remy wanted to wrap his arms around me. I could feel it. Instead, his hand bounced up touching my arm.

"I appreciate that," he said sincerely. "And, I guess I'm not the only one who likes to live dangerously," he said with a smile.

I smiled knowing it was true. "I guess not."

"As the day continued, I introduced Remy to everyone there. With every introduction, it felt increasingly as though I was introducing my boyfriend. I knew he wasn't, and he was never going to be. But, that was the energy between us.

The way Remy looked at me didn't help. It was like he was imagining tossing me onto a bed, flipping me over, and taking what he wanted.

Moreover, the man used every excuse he could to touch me. I mean, I was doing the same, but I wasn't the one planning my wedding; he was. I was the one too foolish to stop falling for a guy planning his wedding. So I was allowed.

Standing in front of everyone after Hil insisted I make a speech, I pondered what I should say. Looking at my mother, who had been talking with Remy's mother, it came to me.

"I would like to thank everyone for being here," I began. "Also, I would like to thank everyone who has agreed to work and volunteer for the center. I was born very close to here. I used to see this building almost every day. I could never have imagined that it would become a place that could make the lives of kids better."

I paused lowering my head as I remembered staring up at the lights, wanting my father to accept me.

"I think it's important for everyone here to know that I'm gay. I'm sure many of you have already figured that out," I said to a few chuckles. I smiled. "I'm not great at hiding it." They laughed again. "But, I thought it was important that I state it. Growing up in this neighborhood, I didn't always believe I could.

"I want this space to be the first of many places in this community where people can feel comfortable saying that. Someone once told me that when you embrace your true self, you are rewarded. Well, I'm gay, and I'm mixed, with a black mother and a white father who wanted nothing to do with me. I don't know why he didn't. But that is the way it was.

"Those things have shaped me. Often, I've run from them. But that is my true self. I want this center to be a place where everyone feels safe being their true selves. Because I believe that if you are true to yourself, life will reward you," I said looking at Remy.

Walking away to a round of applause, I was congratulated by everyone, starting with Hil.

"You never told me about your father," he said.

"You never asked," I responded with a smile.

"It always felt like a topic you didn't want to discuss."

"I guess I didn't." I sighed. "Because it was hard."

"Oh, Dillon," he said, pulling me into a hug. "Have I been a good friend to you?"

"Hil, you have been the best friend I could ever ask for. Thank you for everything you've done for me."

"I don't think I would have survived my life without you," Hil replied, his voice hitching.

"Please don't cry. If you do, I'll be next, and I'll never get through today," I joked.

Hil released me and laughed. "Go do what you have to do. You got this," he said, ushering me off.

By the time things were winding down, the only one I hadn't spoken to was Remy. I had kept him in sight the entire day. He had been his usual charming self. Most of the older ladies and all of the gay guys he spoke to fell in love with him, because, of course, they did. Who wouldn't? And after everyone but the cleanup crew had left, Remy approached me, beaming.

"You were amazing today," he said, giving me that look again.

"Thank you."

"You know, when I suggested you do this, I didn't actually think that you would."

I looked at him, shocked. "You didn't believe in me?" I asked, hitting his arm.

"No, I mean I knew you could. I just didn't think that you would. The only reason I had suggested this was as an excuse to look at you every day."

"Well, that didn't happen," I said, snidely.

"Nope, it did not."

"Nope."

I could see his thoughts swirling. I was about to ask him what he was thinking when he asked,

"Are you ready for your surprise now?"

A flash of excitement shot through me.

"What is it? Did you prepare a fancy dinner for me on the rooftop?" I asked, looking for spoilers.

"No. But that would have been a great idea," he said seriously. "I, um, was just going to split a candy bar with you in my car."

My mouth dropped.

"You said you didn't want me to do anything fancy, didn't you?"

"No, you're right. That's what I said," I agreed, not sure if he was joking.

"So, do you want to have that candy bar now?"

I looked around, wondering if I was being pranked. When I didn't see a camera crew jump out, I returned my gaze to Remy.

"Ah, sure?"

"Great," Remy replied, leading me out. "Don't get me wrong, it's a tasty candy bar. I found it at a specialty store. I think you'll like it."

"Okay," I said, following him across the street to his sleek car.

Getting in, he asked, "Are you ready for this?"

"I guess," I said, trying to hide my disappointment.

Remy reached across my lap and popped open the glove compartment. Staring in as he did, it was empty.

"Oh shit!" he exclaimed with his eyes closed. "I left it on the counter. I can't believe I forgot it. I'm so sorry," Remy said sincerely. "Would you mind terribly if we picked it up? If you don't feel comfortable going back to my place, I could bring it to you tomorrow."

Remy wasn't joking. He was serious. After all his talk about celebrating, this was all he had come up with. If I had known, I would have done something with Hil. How many times would Remy have to disappoint me before I learned?

"I mean, we can get it now," I said, no longer hiding my disappointment.

"We don't have to," he said, seeing the look on my face.

"No, I have nothing else planned," I said pointedly.

"Great," he said with a gentle smile. "I promise you it will be worth it."

"This better be one amazing-tasting candy bar," I muttered, no longer looking at him.

"It will be," he said, starting up his car and pulling off.

As we drove, I stared out the passenger window, lost in thought. How had I allowed myself to fall for him again? He was nothing but heartbreak. It was my own fault. I truly was pathetic.

"We're here," Remy said, snapping me out of my trance.

Looking up, we weren't at his place. We were at the airport. But not LaGuardia or JFK, one for private planes. The car was parked 30 feet from a jet.

"What's going on?" I asked, confused.

Remy looked at me, equally confused. "Oh! You thought I meant my place in New York. No." That was when he dropped his first hint of a smile. "Are you still okay to go?"

I didn't know what to think. "I…"

"Just yes, or no," he said, looking deep into my eyes.

"Yes."

The word was out before I could even think about it.

"Good," he said, getting out of the car and handing its keys to an attendant.

Stopping to offer me his hand at the bottom of the stairs, I looked up at the plane. It wasn't small.

"Remy, what's going on?"

"We're going to get that candy bar. You told me you didn't want me to do anything fancy. So I'm keeping it simple," he said, no longer hiding his devilish smirk.

Warmth filled me realizing that Remy was who I thought he was. Smiling, I took his hand and ascended the steps. Inside was a luxurious cabin decorated with sleek beige leather seats and ambient lighting. Despite its size, it felt intimate and cozy. As I settled into one of the plush chairs, Remy whispered into my ear.

"Get comfortable."

"I suppose you're not going to tell me where we're going," I asked him as he buckled up in the chair across the aisle from mine.

"To get the candy bar," he replied, annoyingly proud of himself.

Once we were in the air, I looked down. We were quickly surrounded by water. I didn't know what to think. Luckily, I didn't have much time to. With the plane leveled off, a flight attendant set up a table in front of me. Once it was stable, Remy took the chair on the other side of it.

"I'm sure you're pretty hungry by now. I hope you don't mind that I arranged for dinner."

"Not at all," I told him before he signaled the steward.

I hadn't been on many planes, so I didn't have much experience with airplane food. But I had no idea that it could be so good. We had a salad named after an emperor, a steak named after a basketball player, and for dessert, ice cream named after a state. Was everything that was served on a plane named after something?

"I don't know, you're coming awfully close to violating the 'fancy' rule."

"What, this? No, this was just what they had in back. Believe me, if they had hot dogs, we would have had that. If nothing else, I'm a man who always follows the rules," he said, charmingly.

I laughed. "Yeah, right. Name a time in your life when you chose to follow the rules."

Remy had to think about it, but he did have an answer. He came up with a few. And what followed was the longest conversation I had ever had with him. To look at him, I would never have guessed how deeply he thought.

"So, what was it like growing up like you did?" I asked.

"What aspect? Do you mean having access to an endless supply of cash because it was stashed in every container in our home? Do you mean, working for my father who was also New York's most feared mafia boss? Or do you mean having to prove myself every day to sharks who could smell blood in the water?"

"Tell me about the girls," I told him, knowing that in all of the years I knew him, he had never once mentioned one.

"Why would you want to talk about that?"

"I don't know. Maybe it turns me on," I suggested flirtatiously.

"Why don't you tell me about your girls?" he said, leaning forward interested.

"I had a great long-term relationship with my mother. And... There, I'm done."

Remy laughed. "Not even one?"

"Ew, no."

"Well, if you get the chance, I recommend pussies."

"For what? Holding my ChapStick? Because that's the only thing I would ever need one for."

Remy laughed again. "So you're not a 'stick-it-in' sort of guy?"

"Do I seem like a 'stick-it-in' sort of guy?"

"You don't," he admitted. "Is that why nothing ever happened between you and Hil? Because neither of you are tops? Or, has something happened?"

"Between Hil and me? No!" I said emphatically. "It would be like having sex with my brother."

"Okay," Remy said, looking relieved.

"But don't dodge the question, Mr. Sneaky. I asked about your girls. I know there's been a lot."

Remy looked pained to talk about them.

"What do you want me to say?"

"Has there been anyone special?" I asked, hiding the terror I felt for his answer.

"No."

"No one?"

"Not really."

"Why not?"

Remy took a deep breath.

"I guess there are a lot of reasons. One was that I never felt comfortable dragging anyone into my world. It's a lot to ask of someone. So, I didn't allow any of them to get too close."

"Hence the charm offensive."

"What do you mean?"

"You're very charming, Remy. Don't pretend you don't know. But it's like the way you always make fun of Cali, isn't it? It's because you don't want to reveal who you really are, which is a soft, caring guy."

"What are you trying to do, get me killed? Because in the world I grew up in, that's what would happen to the guy you described."

My heart broke for Remy.

"What was it like growing up thinking that? It must have been torture."

Remy's eyes drifted away from mine. For the first time, I saw his true self, the one that guarded himself for self-preservation and hated it. His charm was gone. His defenses were down. It was just him, the guy I had gotten glimpses of since I was 14.

"It's not fun," he admitted, showing the strain from the weight he carried.

"I'm sorry," I said, leaning across the table and asking for his hand.

Staring at my hands, I didn't think he was going to take them. But reluctantly, he did. And for a moment, I sat with the man I always knew was buried inside. It was a version of Remy that I loved.

We sat in silence for a while before the attendant offered us drinks, breaking the mood. That was fine because it allowed our conversation to resume. When it did, Remy told me about his hobbies and his favorite TV shows. We even talked about our favorite style of underwear. His was boxer briefs. Yum! Mine was a bikini.

"Nice," he said with enough suggestion that I blushed. "You'll have to model them for me. Maybe you'll get me to switch."

"Maybe I will," I said, feeling the alcohol and wanting his large hands all over me.

By the time the plane descended, it was dark outside. How long had it been?

"Where are we?" I asked, seeing city lights below us. Scanning the landscape, I suddenly knew. "Paris! We're in Paris!"

"Are we?" Remy asked innocently.

"That's the Eiffel Tower!" I exclaimed.

"You sure it's not Vegas?" He asked, teasing my heart.

I quickly turned back to the window. As I did, the plane turned, giving me a better view.

"That's the Arc de Triomphe… and the Louvre," I said, whipping back to face him in excitement.

"Then I guess we're in Paris," he said casually.

I stared at him like a kid on Christmas. I was speechless. He just sat there, pleased with himself. I couldn't decide if I wanted to smack him or tear off his clothes and ride him raw.

Upon landing, there was a car at the airport waiting for us. On the way to wherever we were going, I couldn't stop looking at all the sights whipping by.

"What time is it?" I asked, noting the empty streets.

Remy looked down at his watch.

"5:30 am."

I turned back towards the window. I still couldn't believe what I was seeing. This wasn't my first time out of the country. I had joined Hil and his family on a trip to the Bahamas a few years ago. But because it was so close, it didn't feel foreign. This did. I was practically losing my mind with wonder.

By the time we arrived at an incredible stone building and pulled into an underground parking lot, the sun had started to rise. Taking an elevator to an apartment with a twelve-foot ceiling, wall-sized windows, and a tree-lined balcony that could seat 20 people, we entered.

"There it is!" Remy said, drawing my attention to the candy bar on the coffee table. The table was between the two largest chaise sectionals I had ever seen.

Retrieving it, Remy showed me the red wrapping.

"It's called a Côte d'Or. Would you like a bite?" he asked devilishly.

"I mean, we've come all this way," I said with a smile.

Remy unwrapped it and broke off a piece of the chocolate.

"Close your eyes," he said, approaching me.

I did.

"Now open your mouth. I just want you to focus on the smell and flavor. Nothing else."

As he lifted it to my lips, the chocolate was the last thing I focused on. Instead, I lost myself in the feeling of Remy's warm breath on my skin, and the scent of his faint cologne filling my nostrils. The anticipation it created drove me wild.

When the chocolate touched my tongue, its rich, velvety smoothness melted. The burst of flavors danced in my mouth with the perfect balance of sweet and bitter. It was a symphony of sensations.

"Wow," I whispered, my eyes still closed.

"You like it?" Remy asked softly.

"It's amazing."

"You can open your eyes."

As I did, I found Remy staring at me simmering with desire. The intensity of his gaze sent shivers down my spine. I could do nothing but stare.

"We can head back now if you'd like."

"To New York?" I asked, amused.

"If you want."

"I mean, we're here. It would be a shame to not check out a little of Paris."

"It would be my pleasure to show you around," he said with a rumble in his voice that shook me to my core.

"I would like that," I told him, unable to resist any request he made.

"I'll show you to your room. You should rest up. There's a lot to see."

Entering a door in the middle of the hallway, I stepped into an elegant bedroom with floor-to-ceiling windows and soft lighting that cast a warm glow across the room.

"And where will you be?" I asked, hoping he would say here.

"My room is at the end," he said, leaving me breathless. "You'll find a change of clothes in the closet. You should have everything you need."

"And if I need you?" I asked, staring into his sultry eyes.

"You know where to find me," he said, making me melt as he walked away.

I was ready to explode watching him go. I never wanted anyone more. A part of me wanted to chase him down the hall and mount him like a stallion. Would he have stopped me? Could I stop myself?

Luckily, I didn't have to find out. Disappearing into his room, he closed the door. It was enough to snap the hold he had over me. When it was gone, I retreated to my room.

"How did I end up here?" I asked myself with my heart pounding.

Looking around the room to re-center myself, I couldn't help but notice the luxury: the lush carpet, sturdy furniture, and the view of the enclosed balcony. My breath caught as I took it all in.

Venturing over to the closet, I slowly opened the doors. As soon as I did, I was enveloped in the scent of cedar. It overwhelmed my senses. Closing my eyes and losing myself, it relaxed me.

Opening my eyes calmer, I explored the clothes in front of me. There was something for every occasion. Running my fingers over them, it all felt expensive. The suits' wool, the shirts' silk, even the casual pants felt unexpectedly soft. More than that, everything was in my size.

Turning from the closet to the bed, I was equally impressed. Not only was it so large that I would have to climb onto it, but the sheet floated above the mattress as if wrapping a marshmallow. It looked amazingly comfortable. And unable to resist, I jumped on it feeling the rush of wind tickle my ears as the duvet settled around me.

I didn't think it would be possible to fall asleep with all the excitement coursing through me, but I guess I was wrong. As my muscles released and my mind let go, the exhaustion from the grand opening, plane ride, and time difference took over. As my eyelids grew heavy, I didn't fight it. I had made it to the one place I had always wanted to be. And with my heart growing fuller, I let go of my thoughts and succumbed to sleep.

When I awoke, the first thing I felt was a rush of panic. How much time had passed? Shooting out of bed in a flurry, I exited my room headed to Remy's. Hearing a spoon in a coffee cup, I changed directions. Reentering the living room, I found Remy sitting on the couch near the balcony engrossed in a book. Looking up and seeing me, he stared at me concerned.

"Dillon, what's wrong?" He asked ready to hurry to me.

"I slept the day away," I said in distress. "I missed everything!"

Remy smiled at me with a warmth in his eyes that melted my anxiety.

"Relax, Dillon. Nothing important happens in Paris before noon," he told me, calming my heart. "We still have the whole day ahead of us."

I exhaled a shaky breath feeling a slight embarrassment for my overreaction. Remy laughed.

"Don't laugh. I was worried," I told him sincerely.

"I know you were. That's what makes it funny," Remy said devilishly.

I huffed at his teasing and in return, he held out his arms.

"Ahh! Come here," he said calling me to him.

Maybe I was still groggy. Maybe something else was going on. But in either case, seeing his arms wide, I crawled into them. Cuddling up to him, he held me. I could have stayed there forever.

"Two questions," I said when the excitement of being in Paris drew me back.

"What's that?"

"One, you read? Two, since when do you read?"

I looked up at Remy who smiled. Flipping the hardcover in his hands, he said, "Yes, I read, and I've always read. My nap was shorter than yours so I decided to grab a coffee and see if I could get through anymore of my French reading list."

I stared at Remy.

"How have I never seen you read before?"

"You haven't seen me do a lot of things. For example, did you know that I also shower?"

"I've seen you do that," I told him casually.

"What? When did you see me shower?"

"Your family's casual attitude toward locking your bathroom doors is astounding," I told him remembering all of the times I walked in on him and Hil.

Remy chuckled. "I guess it is. We're French."

"I mean, kind of. I don't know if you can claim to be French if you grow up in America. The way I see it, you're as American as I am. And Americans lock the bathroom door."

Remy laughed. "I'll have to remember that."

"I said they do. I didn't say you should," I clarified flirtatiously.

"Oh, and why shouldn't I?"

"I don't know. What if there's an emergency or something?" I explained.

"An emergency? Like what?"

"What if someone needs to see you in the shower? How would they do that if the door's locked?" I asked as my body washed in heat.

"I guess they would have to ask. All they would need to do is ask," he said staring down into my eyes.

I swallowed wondering if this was going to be it. It had been hard not to think about our kiss every moment since it happened. But I had had the grand opening to distract me. After that, I had been whisked away on a private jet to Paris. Now, all of that was behind me. In front of me was Remy with his sparkling eyes and his soft pink lips.

"We should grab something to eat," I told him calling on all of my self-restraint.

As much as I wanted him, and that was a lot, I couldn't forget that he wasn't mine. Whether he wanted to be or not, he was engaged and I didn't want to be that person. I didn't want to be his afterthought.

"Are you hungry?" Remy asked loosening his grip on me.

"Yeah," I said feeling him pull away and immediately wondering if I had made a mistake not kissing him.

"I know the perfect place," he said gesturing for me to get up. "Did you want to shower first?" he asked with a smirk.

"I should," I told him standing.

"And will that bathroom door be unlocked," he asked suggestively.

Pantomiming locking a door, I turned and walked away. I have no idea why I did that. Sure, I thought it would be funny since I mentioned what I had about Americans. But the last thing I wanted him to think was that he wouldn't be welcome in my shower.

Or would he be? I asked myself as I retreated to my room and entered the attached private bath. Undressing, I stared into the wide oval mirror that curved towards me on either end. I stared at my lean body naked. Pushing my hand across my chest, I imagined what Remy's large hands would look like contrasted to my tan skin.

It made me hard. Taking hold of my cock I squeezed imagining it was Remy doing it. My head fell back from pleasure.

With my eyes closed I pictured Remy leaning down and kissing my lips. He was gentle but assertive. And when I opened my mouth, his tongue entered.

Standing behind me naked, I could feel his large cock. It would be even bigger than what I had seen when I had walked in on him when I was a kid. And testing my opening, he would slide in as if I were made for him.

Stroking my cock, I imagined Remy doing it as he fucked me. I groaned from the pleasure. He was so big. Everything about him made me feel so small.

Lifting me in the air, my legs would fold back around his. And losing myself to the rhythm of his thrusts, he would fuck me harder and harder until he bit my shoulder and I exploded.

"Ahh," I moaned, hearing the tone echoed back to me in the large, sparse room.

Catching my breath, I leaned forward, bracing myself on the sink. My mind was crackling. I wanted desperately to bury myself in his arms. But as the real world returned to me, my reality reemerged.

Opening my eyes, the first thing I saw was myself in the mirror. The yearning boy looking back at me made me sad. For so long, no one had loved him. He had had hookups with guys in college, but he had never been more than a warm body to them.

There had only ever been two people who had claimed to care more. But past Hil and my mother, no one did. I could get lost in the streets of Paris and never return, and only two people would ever miss me.

Looking down at the trails of my pleasure, I quickly cleaned it up and headed to the freestanding tub with its attached hand shower. As the water worked its way through my thick curls to my scalp, I reconsidered what I had just thought.

Could I disappear and never come back? That might have been true before yesterday, but I had just opened the community center. Was it true anymore?

As the warm water layered my body, I thought about what would happen if I disappeared and never returned to the center. Yes, I had put in place everyone necessary to run it without me, but I still had responsibilities. People were depending on me. Whether or not I returned, mattered.

I let that thought roll around in my mind. It was a new way of looking at myself. For so long, I didn't matter to anybody. Not even my father cared if I lived. But that wasn't true anymore. I was needed… and it felt good.

Remy had given me this. The job, the clothes, the luxury apartment, none of it compared to this gift. And he probably didn't even know what he had done.

Finishing up, I toweled off and got dressed. When I returned to the living room, it was just in time to see him exit his bedroom. How was it that there was suddenly something about him that made him look even hotter? He had been gorgeous before, but now, all I could do was bite my lip and hope he didn't notice the bulge growing in my pants.

"You look refreshed," he said, staring at me amused. "How was the shower? Good?"

"Yeah," I said, struggling to speak.

"Nice! As you could probably guess, my door was unlocked, you know, in case of an emergency. I guess no emergencies came up."

I giggled like a ten-year-old. He noticed and laughed heartily. I had to pull myself together. I might be an idiot, but I didn't have to act like it.

"I mean, the place wasn't on fire, so…" I said, trying to regain my self-respect and failing.

"Am I going to have to burn the place down to get you in there? Okay. Well, remind me to pick up some matches later."

I giggled in reply. Okay, now he was just making me giggle on purpose. Was he getting a sick pleasure from watching me humiliate myself? He was such an asshole, such a gorgeous, irresistible asshole.

"Food," I said, changing the topic with the only word I could force out of my mouth.

"Right! And again, I know the perfect place," he told me with a smile.

Like I said, the guy was an asshole. Because the place he chose was a café overlooking the river. Sitting outside, we shared French toast, and a basket of croissants while sipping our coffees. It was like a movie. And every second that passed, I fell more in love with him.

Leaving the café, Remy led me to the famous Champs-Élysées, where he insisted we do some shopping. I thought he meant for himself until we entered the most expensive-looking store I had ever seen and he said,

"Let's find you something bold. You always dress so conservatively. You need something that will catch everyone's eye. They need to see you the way I do," he said, guiding me through a high-end store on Avenue Montaigne that made my wallet weep.

"This," he said, selecting a jacket and pants from a rack.

"No shirt?" I asked, looking around at the selection.

"With a body like yours?" he bemused. "It would be a waste. Go," he said, ushering me off.

Trying on that outfit and others, and then modeling them for him, I felt like a doll. Each time he ran his hand down the seams checking its fit, my heart pounded. He had to know what he was doing to me, didn't he?

Standing there not being able to touch him back was torture. And the way he looked at me when he found an outfit he liked put thoughts in my head of him pushing me into the dressing room, stripping me bare, and having his way with me.

"Perhaps these glasses, to show off your intellectual side," he suggested, as he leaned in and put a pair of lightly tinted sunglasses on my face. His scent wafted over me. My knees weakened feeling his breath on my cheek.

"Or this jacket to showcase that tiny waist of yours," he continued, engulfing my sides with his large, powerful hands.

Staring up at him in the mirror, his annoyingly charming smirk flashed back. Yep, he knew exactly what he was doing to me. Well, screw him, I wasn't going to give in to it. I would resist everything. I would create a wall between the two of us that was fifty feet tall. I would not let him in.

But, with every moment we spent together, my resolve crumbled. With every touch, being disconnected from Remy became unbearable. I was headed towards dangerous territory, and I couldn't stop myself. So when we left the shops with the sun streaming beautiful streaks of yellow and orange across the Paris streets, I slipped my fingers between his.

It was enough to quiet the aching screams in my head. For that brief time, I had him. He was mine. It was all I would allow myself with the taken man beside me. And for the moment, it was just enough.

"This is one of my favorite spots," Remy said as we approached a casual, yet busy restaurant for dinner.

"What makes it your favorite?" I asked, wanting to know everything about him.

"I don't know. It's unpretentious."

I chuckled. "I thought you liked pretentious."

"Me? Are you joking? All I need is a bottle of Château Pétrus Pomerol and a little Époisses de Bourgogne on a cracker and I couldn't be happier." Remy paused. "Okay, I heard it. But I still deny it."

"Ahh, the poor little rich boy can't acknowledge his privilege," I teased.

That flustered him. "I brought you here for the French Onion soup. What could be less pretentious than that?"

"Than French Onion soup?" I asked, stunned. "How about anything?"

"But we're in France. Here it's just called onion soup."

I looked at him and shook my head. He was so clueless that it was adorable. And as I ate what had to be the most incredible soup of my life, I was entertained watching the big baby seated across from me pout.

He was still pouting as we left the restaurant and headed for dessert.

"You okay there?" I asked, taking his hand again.

"Did you see how much cheese I added to the soup? I'm not pretentious. I couldn't be more basic if I tried."

"Remy, you asked for a side of Gruyère," I pointed out.

"And? That's the cheese they put in Onion soup."

I laughed. "Remy, you're pretentious. Accept it. Why does it even bother you?"

"Because I don't want there to be a distance between us."

"A distance? What do you mean?"

"I don't want there to be a part of my life that you don't feel comfortable in," he said, drawing my hand around his arm.

"Maybe it's okay if we aren't exactly the same. Maybe our differences are what the other needs. And by being our true selves with each other, we'll each reach a place we couldn't by ourselves," I said vulnerably.

"So, you're saying there's a "we"?" Remy replied, cockily.

"Did you not hear anything else I just said?"

"Nope! But I've confirmed there is a "we". Did you say anything after that?" he asked, pleased with himself.

I rolled my eyes and shook my head. "Men!"

"Don't you love 'em?" Remy teased.

"Barely!" I joked.

Getting a sampling of desserts, we dipped in and out of the street lights, finding our way back to the Seine. Walking the cobblestones next to the river as the din of the city faded into the background, the two of us lost ourselves exploring the sweets. Each was better than the next. And by the time it was all gone, we were both full and quiet.

"I couldn't have imagined a better day," I told him as the street lights twinkled on the rippling water.

"This might be my favorite day ever," Remy admitted, not looking at me as he did.

"What's wrong?" I asked him, pulling his arm against me.

"We should head back. There are things I want to show you in the morning and neither of us has had much sleep."

"I'm not sure that sleep is in my future anytime soon. Are you sure you don't want to stop at a bar for a sampling of French wine?" I asked, not wanting the day to end.

He turned to look at me. Sadness filled his eyes. I didn't understand. Where was the endless flirt who had driven me crazy all day?

"No. We should call it a night. But, tomorrow," he said with melancholy.

"Sure," I said, hiding my disappointment.

Was it happening again? Had he made me fall for him before pulling the rug out from under me?

No. I wasn't going to go there. There was more to Remy than a flirt or tease. Over the past few months, he had done more for me than I could dream of. If his mood had changed, or if he decided that he no longer wanted to be with me, there had to be a good reason for it.

I wasn't going to let it hurt me. But I could also no longer doubt that he cared about me. I had to let him be him.

"You're not upset, are you?" Remy asked, telling me how poorly I was hiding how I felt.

"Remy, even if I was, wait a minute, it'll change."

"Your feelings and the weather, huh?"

I smiled painfully, acknowledging that it was true.

With that, Remy wrapped his arm around me, pulling me tight. It was a nice consolation prize. Walking back to his exquisite apartment, he held my face between his hands and looked longingly into my eyes.

Heat washed across my body. I couldn't tell if it was coming from him or me. In either case, I could see that he wanted me as much as I wanted him. Then why wasn't he leaning down? Why wasn't he kissing me?

"Goodnight," he said, touching his lips to my forehead.

"Goodnight," I told him, doing my best to muster a smile before he let me go and disappeared into his room.

I quietly listened. Had he locked the door? It didn't sound like he had. Was that my invitation? I didn't think it was.

Disappointed, I headed to my bedroom, got undressed, and went to bed. I dreamt of Remy. In the dream, he tested my doorknob. Finding it unlocked, he entered finding me naked and asleep.

Unable to resist the sight, he climbed on top of me and consumed my body. Watching him do it as if my body were someone else's, I ached for him. And the screams the two made as he dominated it, drove me wild.

Opening my eyes alone in my bed, my heart pounded. Rolling over to escape the morning light, I found that my sheets were wet. My god, it was like I was again 14 years old dreaming of the only boy I ever did.

Remy had always been the only boy I ever wanted. I genuinely ached for the man.

It was then that I realized something. Taken or not, I would never be able to stop feeling the way I did about him. I had to accept that.

As I did, I forgave my mother. I had grown up resenting her for being with my father, a married man. But now I understood. Her decision was neither good nor right, but I finally got why she made it.

Lying in bed wondering what I was going to do, I stared at the intricate inlay on the ceiling. I lost myself in it. When I re-emerged, it was to thoughts of sharing my bed with Remy. I imagined the two of us staring up at the ceiling together. My chest clenched thinking about it.

This hurt too much. I needed to get up. Climbing out of bed, I stood in front of the sliding glass door to the balcony, allowing the morning light to touch my naked skin.

Staring out, I admired the wooden deck encircled by plush sectional patio furniture. I wished I could go out and lay bare in the sun. I might have if more than one side had been a wall of trees.

On the other hand, weren't the French less hung up on nudity than Americans were? If someone walked onto their balcony and saw me lounging nude, would they care?

Deciding it was better not to find out, I instead headed to the closet. Opening it, I was surprised to find the outfits I had tried on the day before added to the selection. When had Remy even purchased them, much less had them sent here?

Choosing the one that Remy reacted strongest to, I got dressed and headed to the living room excited to see his reaction.

"Good morning," he said with a smile as his eyes rolled over me.

"Morning," I replied, pleased with his reaction.

"Sleep well?"

Remembering my dream, my cheeks flushed. "I guess," I said, weighing it against the restlessness it had created. "How about you?"

"It was a mixed bag," he admitted.

"How come?"

"I kept thinking about you all night," he said, returning to his flirtatious ways.

I stared at him. "You know, if you keep talking like that, you better be prepared with some follow-up, Mister," I said, placing my body inches from his.

I was expecting him to kiss me. At least, I was hoping he would. But instead, he dropped his charm offensive and calmly said, "Noted."

I was disappointed. Did this mean that his flirtation had always just been an act?

"I think I have a pretty good day planned," he said casually walking away. My chest ached watching him go.

"Oh yeah? Care to share?"

"Are you the type who likes to know how a story will end or be surprised?"

I thought about that. It was a good question. If I knew that nothing would ever happen between the two of us, would I want to know that?

"Surprise me," I told him, mustering a smile.

"Okay," he said, faintly smiling back.

Gathering our stuff, we headed to a restaurant. Our breakfast was salmon and a fried egg on a doughnut. Wow!

From there we went to a museum called Orsay. In it were paintings I had heard of my entire life. Van Gogh, Monet, and Gauguin had all just been names. But now, there their paintings were in front of us. And we were taking selfies with them acting goofy.

From there we walked through the museum's traveling exhibition. It featured the painting "The Scream" which I'm pretty sure was mentioned on 'Sesame Street'. It hurt my brain considering that I was now somehow standing in front of it.

As captivating as everything was, by the time we left the museum, it was late. A whole day had flown by. Initially, I had felt overdressed and self-conscious among the tourists. But I quickly lost myself in the artwork. There was so much more beauty in the world than I had ever considered.

"Thank you for showing me that," I told Remy as we exited past the giant clock and five-story wall of windows that were reminiscent of Grand Central Station.

"I thought you'd like that," he said with a smile.

"Considering it was kind of pretentious, I'm assuming it's one of your favorite spots?" I teased.

Remy blushed. "It is."

I smiled. "Now it's one of mine, too."

Remy looked down at me, moved. It was then that he took my hand. He had never done that before. I had taken his, and he had kissed me, but never before had he done something so intimate. I liked it. I wanted more.

"Where to next?" I said, never wanting this day to end.

"Spoilers," he said, looking pleased with himself.

When we got there, I had to admit that his cockiness was well-deserved. Because there it was before us, France's most iconic symbol, the Eiffel Tower. I was dumbstruck.

It looked exactly like it did in pictures. And with the sun set, its lights set it aglow.

Staring at it, a tear streamed down my cheek. I didn't know why I was crying, but I was. Everything was just so perfect. Not taking my eyes off of it, I rested my head on his shoulder.

"Thank you," I whispered, unable to say anything else.

"You're welcome," he replied, pulling me into his arms.

I couldn't take it anymore, I had to kiss him. I needed to be closer to him. So, with my heart thumping and my fist tightening, I was about to pull him down to me when…

"What was that? What's going on?" I said as the Eiffel Tower began to twinkle.

"That's for us," he said.

"What?"

"I told them to let me know when our table was ready. There it is," he said, gesturing towards the tower.

"No you didn't," I said, no longer knowing what to believe.

"There it is," he said, gesturing again. "Our table's ready."

"Our table where?"

He smiled.

Riding the elevator up to the restaurant within the Eiffel Tower was incredible on its own. The view from the restaurant, however, was breathtaking.

Seated next to the window, Paris was sparkling beneath us. I could barely look away. When I did, it was to Remy's smiling face.

"The first time I came here was as a kid with my family," he said drawing my attention. "I couldn't appreciate it. I have to admit, experiencing it now through your eyes, I'm starting to see how much I missed. I'm starting to learn that privilege has its disadvantages."

I wanted to argue with him but I couldn't. What must it be like to take views like this one for granted? When your life is so amazing that you can't appreciate this, what room does that leave for wonder?

For the first time since meeting the gorgeous man across from me, I felt sorry for him. It wasn't in a mean way. It was more that I felt sympathy.

He wasn't a god no matter how much he resembled the sculptures of them at the museum. He was just a man full of hopes, dreams, and fears. Perhaps the gods were the same. Maybe, that is all any of us are no matter how much power or money we have.

I reached across the table asking for Remy's hand. He gave it to me. I loved him for it. I didn't let it go until the waiter brought our meal, all four courses of it.

"That was incredible," I told him, happier than I had ever been.

"I'm glad you liked it. It's tradition to end things with a dessert wine. Interested?"

I considered it. "Yes. Did I see some on the wine shelf at your place?"

"Good eye. You did."

"I hadn't. I just guessed," I admitted.

Remy chuckled. "Good guess. Would you like to go back and try a little of it?"

"I think I'd like that," I told him, never wanting him to leave my sight.

"Then we should go," he said, his cheeks glowing.

Exiting the restaurant and entering the elevator, he took my hand. Heat washed through me. I felt electric. Dressed as I was, there was no hiding what he did to me. My neck and exposed chest glowed calling for his touch. My pounding heart begged for his kiss.

When the cool breeze of nightfall tickled my warm skin, I shivered. I couldn't think. My brain stopped working. The only thing I could do was follow his lead and I was going to. Because as the tingles danced around my balls making me hard, I knew I could no longer resist him.

With my heart racing as his apartment door closed behind us, I couldn't breathe. When he turned giving me a smoldering look, I stared back. I was about to pounce.

"Wine?" he asked leaving me for the kitchen.

"Yeah," I said breathless.

Unable to budge, I watched him. He moved effortlessly. Grabbing a bottle and two glasses, he led me to the couch. Sitting, I was on fire.

"What do we toast to?" he asked a low rumble to his voice that vibrated my taint.

I giggled. It was all I could do. Remy chuckled in reply.

Handing me a glass, he filled it. Filling his own, he said, "You know, Dillon, you always make it hard on me."

I paused. "How?"

"I've always known my destiny. I was the firstborn son and a Lyon. My future was set. But from the moment I met you, I've wanted to be a good person. I've wanted to be worthy of you. And then I would have to do things I knew weren't."

"You're a good person," I forced out.

"I'm not. And the problem is that I know I'm not. I could have walked away from the family business sooner. I could have made better decisions once I realized that you made me crazy enough to rip doors off of walls. And now, knowing what a good person should do, I want to hold you so badly that I would burn the world to have you. I…"

And that was when I kissed him. Throwing my body on top of him, our lips pressed. With my gesture, Remy was released.

Taking over, I felt his strength beneath me. Wrapping his arms around me, he gripped the back of my head. Rolling me over and pushing my back against the couch, he tightened our bodies together and opened my mouth.

As his heat enveloped me, his tongue searched for mine. Quickly finding it, he invited it to dance. My head spun as they twirled on one another. And when his other hand gripped my ass and squeezed, I squeaked in pleasure.

I wanted him. I needed him. Digging my fingertips into his back, I pulled at his shirt. I had to get it off. And when I lifted it enough that he couldn't ignore it, he let me go long enough to remove it.

Pulling it over his head, he released my lips. His body was gone for just a flash before he returned but it was enough. I could see that his chest was perfect. The ripples of his abs rivaled an ocean. And the chiseling of his chest crumbled marble. I was drunk for his body.

Wrapping my legs around his torso with our kiss reignited, he picked me up. My skin burned to touch his. Desperately pulling our chests together, the sensation was everything I had dreamed of.

When the plush comforter sprung up around us, I relaxed onto the mattress. Climbing on top of me, he pulled away long enough to remove my jacket. As he did, he admired my body.

"Beautiful," he said staring down at me.

My breath hitched. I had become addicted to his touch. Writhing under him, I tugged at the comforter needing to connect with him again. He saw me squirm and smirked.

"Tell me you want me," he demanded.

I couldn't speak. I wanted him. I wanted everything about him. But nothing left my mouth.

His gaze burned into me waiting until he said, "Say it or not, I'm gonna fuck you," he declared making my body flinch.

That was when he did it. Taking ownership of my body, he placed his fingertips on my bare chest. His power was immense. He was pinning me to the mattress without effort. I couldn't escape if I wanted to.

With my movements tamed, he lightened his touch and traced a path across my abs. He messaged the dips. He liked what he felt. His pleasure was my drug.

Not stopping there, his fingertip reached the waist of my pants. I couldn't breathe. Hovering, he tugged at it. What was he going to do, unbutton them? Stop?

It was neither. Without permission, he continued further. Knowing where he was going, my cock flinched. I closed my eyes feeling every sensation.

He didn't go right for it. Pressing the cloth around it, I felt his closeness. I tensed my dick needing him to touch it. He refused.

Tracing its outline instead, my mind screamed for him to take me. When he finally did, it was with aggression. It was like his damn had broken. He was through messing around. He was taking what was his.

Squeezing it and pressing it against my body, I moaned. I needed to feel his warm flesh around my cock. So when he finally unlatched and unzipped my pants, I melted into the bed as my dick sprung out.

As his lips wrapped around my cock, I found heaven. This was what I had dreamed of for so long. Remy Lyon's mouth was swallowing my dick and it was everything to me.

With his hands clutching my balls, the tip of his tongue traversed the rim of my head. I could barely stand it. Tearing into the sheets, my toes stretched.

Lowering his head, he swallowed it and then resurfaced. Needing more, he did it again. Back and forth, he danced with it. He seemed to like doing it as much as I enjoyed it. And when his strokes got me close enough to cum, he released me, stripped the both of us, and slid up my body.

With the back of my thighs pressed against his chest, my hips lifted. Leaning down to kiss me, he parted my lips. His tongue wasn't the only thing of his that wanted in me, his tip searched for my opening. When it found my hole, it perched.

What was he doing? What was he waiting for? Pinned under him, I couldn't move. I was at his mercy. I ached for him.

So when he braced his hands on either side of my head and pushed, I whimpered. It hurt but it felt good. I had seen him naked. He was big. But pushing into me, he felt huge.

Expecting Remy to be merciful, he wasn't. He was taking me. With his cock tearing me apart, I met the real Remy, the part of him he had hidden.

This Remy was dominating and relentless. I would have squirmed away if I could, but he wouldn't let me. I was his to do with what he pleased. I was clay in his large, powerful hands and he was going to reshape me in his impressive image.

Pushing inside of me, I groaned. I could feel every inch. Planted within me, my opening molded around the ridge of his helmet and every bulging vein. My ass was no long mine. He owned it. And now that he had it, he did what he told me he would, he fucked me.

Slow at first, his pace increased. As big as he was, his groin still slapped my ass. He was deep inside of me, but having reshaped around him, I fit him like a glove.

Losing myself as the tingle crawled up my thigh, my eyes rolled. I was cumming. By the sound of him, so was he. We were cumming together and I wasn't even touching my cock. It was happening from his thrusts alone.

Breathing harder, my chest clenched with my balls and dick to follow.

"Ahh," I moaned.

I couldn't hold it back. There was a shot of electricity tearing its way through me. Burying my nails into his back, I scratched. He peeled away beneath me. And when my screams reached a crescendo, so did his.

The firehose released within me mirrored the one that covered us both. I couldn't stop cumming. The flinching was spasmic.

Exhausted, Remy's body collapsed onto mine. My cock continued to twitch. This was the greatest sexual experience of my life and I didn't want it to end.

Drunk from pleasure, I wrapped my arms around my man. I never wanted to be a part from him again. I never would be. I wouldn't let it.

I loved him. I always had. And that was when I heard the words that ripped my heart out changing the direction of my life.

Chapter 11

Remy

I couldn't believe it. I was lying naked on the man of my dreams with my still hard cock in his ass. How many times had I fantasized about this? There had been weeks after meeting him that he was the first thing I thought of when I woke up and the last thing I thought about before falling asleep.

For so long, he had been my everything. And now, here we were. I had him. He was mine. I no longer knew how to live without him.

I was ready to run away with him. Anywhere he wanted to go, I wanted to take him. I was more than happy to leave everything behind.

Fuck my responsibilities, my obligations. There was nothing that mattered more to me than Dillon. With him in my arms, my life felt complete.

"Remy!" I heard her say from the doorway behind me.

The second I heard it, my chest clenched. My dream had lasted as long as it had taken me to cum.

"What the fuck, Remy?" she said robbing me of strength.

Quickly shrinking out of Dillon, darkness blinded me as I rolled over and faced reality naked.

"What the fuck are you doing here?" I said staring at my fiancé.

"What the fuck am I doing here? What are you? Are fucking him? After all of the times you told me that nothing was going on between you two, and how he was just your charity case…"

Her words were water on molten steel. Boiling, ready to explode, I shot out of bed onto my feet. Pointing at her wanting to rip her head off I growled, "I never said that. I never called him my charity case. Never!"

"Alright," she said backing off realizing she had made a mistake. "Your brother's boyfriend, or whatever."

"I've never talked to you about Dillon. Don't you dare pretend like I have," I said happy to do whatever it took to set the record straight.

"Fine. You didn't talk about him. But that doesn't give you permission to run off somewhere and fuck him in the ass."

I retreated.

"I mean look at you. I walk in finding you fucking him and you have the nerve to say something to me."

"I don't owe you anything," I said thrown off balance by the situation.

"You owe me everything! As far as you're concerned, your life and the life of everyone you care about is in my hands. Who do you think my father will kill first when I tell him about this, huh? You think it might be the trash I found your dick in?"

"Don't call him that," I said again ready to explode.

"Or, maybe your brother? Or your mother? Or do you think that he'll just hire someone to murder the whole lot of you and be done with it? You've met my father. Which of those things do you think he's not capable of?"

As much as I hated her, I knew she was telling the truth. Her father was a psychopath. I knew it because no matter how much my father loved his family, he was too. Nothing stood in the way of him getting what he wanted and his vengeance was that of legend.

"Yeah, that's what I thought," Eris said when she knew that she had me.

I was willing to sacrifice my life for anyone Eris had mentioned, especially Dillon. But I wasn't willing to risk a hair on his head to save myself.

To protect them, my sentence had to be life. I hated it, but it was true. There was no way out of this without someone dying. And if I was the one doing the killing, I would have to do it at the expense of being with Dillon.

Dillon thought he knew who I was. But what he didn't… couldn't know, was that I was a Lyon. I had come from my father's blood. I was capable of doing what my father had and more. I was sure of it.

I had never allowed myself to go there. Dreaming of one day having a life with Dillon had held me back. I never wanted to cross the line to become a man he could never be with. And to free myself of my sentence, that was who I would have to become.

With the barred doors closing on me, would I become that man now? It would be so easy. Who even knew that Eris was here? With her gone, I would have the jump on her father. In hours, his empire could be mine. I could be the most feared man in New York. And all it would cost would be the way Dillon looked at me.

I looked back at the beautiful man laying scared in my bed. His large eyes, his creamy skin, I needed them to breath. The price of my freedom was too high. Realizing it, my head drooped.

"Here's what's going to happen," Eris began. "Look at me."

Without thinking, I turned to her.

"Since I'm not a monster, I'm going to give you an hour. When that hour is done, you're going to say goodbye to him and then you will never see him again. Ever! Do you understand me?"

Staring at her, I wanted to snap her neck. I didn't. Instead, I looked away defeated.

"Good. See, I can be reasonable. I have a heart. But, don't mistake sympathy for weakness because that's how people end up dead. Tell me you understand."

I refused to look at her.

"And you, you tell me you understand."

The second I realized she was talking to Dillon, I reacted.

"Don't you talk to him!"

"It's okay, Remy. I think I finally understand," he said looking at me with sadness in his eyes.

"It's about time," Eris quipped sarcastically. "Now I'll leave you two to it. And when it's done, I look forward to starting the rest of my life with my soon-to-be husband," she said taking a quick look down at my naked body and smiling.

With her words cutting me to shreds, I couldn't look as she exited. Waiting to hear the main door open and close, I found myself bound within the chains created by thinking I could for once have what I wanted.

The silence between Dillon and me drew out. I was too ashamed to look at him. Had I made the right choice not to kill her? Was I making the correct choice now?

"It's not your fault, Remy," Dillon's soft voice said.

"It's all my fault," I countered.

"How? Tell me how any of this is your fault," Dillon insisted.

I looked at him wondering how this could even be a question.

"I could have done more."

"Of what?"

"I don't know. More."

"Remy, you didn't ask to be born to the man you were, just like I didn't. We're both children of fate, cursed to pay for the sins of our fathers."

Was that true? Could that be why I had felt like I had known him back when all I knew was his name?

Dillon's mouth opened as if making a final request. "Please lie with me. If we only have an hour left to be together, let me spend it in your arms," he said breaking my heart.

I stared at him from the foot of the bed. "I don't want it to end like this. I won't let it."

"Then, I will. I'll end it. Not because I'm scared of what her father would do to me. But because I'm scared of what he would do to you... and Hil, and your mother. I can't be the cause of you all getting hurt. I can't," he said with tears in his eyes.

"I wouldn't let it..."

"Please," he said cutting me off. "Just lie with me. Let's finish making this the perfect night," he said wiping his face with the back of his hand.

Without another word, I crawled back into bed and pulled my naked love into my arms. He fit perfectly. With his arms balled in front of him, my wings covered him making the two of us one.

As the hour passed, we didn't speak. When our time was done, he graciously pulled away and looked for his clothes. To my surprise, he seemed accepting of everything.

"Did you tell her you were coming here?" he asked as he collected his underwear and pulled them on.

"Of course not," I said drinking in every inch of him hoping to remember it for a lifetime.

"Then how did she know where to find us?"

How did she know?

"Oh fuck!" I exclaimed looking at my wrist.

"The watch," Dillon said coming to the same conclusion.

"That fucking bitch put a tracker in it," I said rushing to my feet, yanking it off, and smashing it with a marble orb which until that moment had served no purpose.

With it pulverized to broken glass, Dillon asked me, "Do you think it was a fake?"

"I had it checked. It was real."

"So, you just destroyed two million dollars?"

"Yep," I confirmed not giving two shits.

"Okay," he said staring at me fully dressed. "So, I guess this is it?"

"Is it ever "it" between the two of us?" I asked with a smile.

"Yes. Because this time it isn't you saying it, it's me," he said fighting for courage. "It's over. I never want to see you again. Never," he said softly breaking my heart.

And with that, he walked out of my bedroom and my life while I stood naked watching him.

The pounding pain in my chest wouldn't cease. I stared at the closed bedroom door as Dillon's departure echoed through the room. Memories of him trailed throughout my apartment like his soft lingering scent.

As much as I wanted to wallow in it, to lose myself completely in the memory of him, I couldn't. It wasn't over. It couldn't be. My heart refused to accept it.

Within the room's deafening silence, a name flashed through my mind. Lucien had been the closest thing I had to a friend growing up. He lived in Paris and might be the only person who could understand what I was going through.

Grabbing my phone, I dialed his now seldom-used number.

"Hell of a time to call, Remy," Lucien's cool voice hummed lightening the tension cinched tightly around my chest.

"How about grabbing a drink?" I asked desperately trying to escape the echoes of Dillon's goodbye.

"Le Bar Diamant?" Lucien volunteered with genuine warmth just like the old days.

"With pleasure," I murmured, hanging up.

I threw on a white shirt and dark jeans and got out of there. Entering Le Bar Diamant, I looked around. The bar was wrapped in velvety darkness.

Seeing my cousin for the first time in years, I got his attention. Heading over, we hunkered down at a corner table. The hum of conversations surrounding us blanketed us in solitude. Being handed a glass as soon as I sat down, I took a swig and stared at my old friend.

"I hear you're getting hitched," Lucien started, swirling the amber liquid in his tumbler.

"Got backed into a corner," I admitted before taking another drink.

His sharp green eyes studied me. I could see his empathy shimmering beneath the hardened surface of our mafia upbringing. Seeing my discomfort, Lucien switched topics.

"I might have something that can take your mind off of these things," he said, his voice taking a mysterious turn.

"What's that?"

"I know of an auction tonight. It will be a bit unusual. It could help you get some perspective," Lucien suggested with a hint of mischief sparkling in his eyes.

The way Lucien had proposed the idea made me pause. But what harm could a little frivolity do? It might feel good to spend an evening pretending that my world hadn't come crashing around me? After all, wasn't that why I had called Lucien?

I gulped down the remainder of my drink.

"Alright. Let's go," I told him intrigued and desperate for a diversion.

Following my cousin out of the bar and into the cool Parisian night, eventually we arrived at the auction. Apparently, Lucien had left a few things out. Entering the heavy metal warehouse doors, I realized that this wasn't the type of auction that got advertised. Even so, spilling into a dimly lit room, the awaiting crowd consisted of only the richest and most spoilt within French society.

Turning to my cousin to find out what was going on, he appeared tense. His green eyes jumped from person to person as if searching for someone.

Watching him warily, the knot in my stomach churned. This was a side of Lucien I hadn't seen before. His quiet intensity and strange restlessness made him look more like a predator preparing to pounce on its prey.

The crowd's mummers fell silent as the auction began. When the first items were presented, I understood what was going on. The indigenous masks and centuries-old swords weren't exactly pieces that could be sold at a respectable auction house. Because even if they weren't stolen from a museum, they had to have been taken from their cultural homes without the permission of the native people.

Watching Lucien as the items got more interesting, he didn't move. The carefree nature that was on display just an hour earlier was gone. In its place was a deadly seriousness I didn't recognize within my friend. And when the gasps from the night's final prize filled the room, my cheerful cousin changed.

Turning back to the auction stand, I saw it. The auction's last item was a Bengal tiger. Pacing back and forth in its cage, it looked as dangerous as it did scared.

I couldn't take my eyes off of it, it was astonishing. Its majesty was devastatingly misplaced in the seedy world it had found itself. And turning back to Lucien in search of his thoughts, I saw as my cousin's focus hardened.

With each new bid his eyes zeroed in on the bidder. I could practically see his calculations. This was why he had come. He hadn't brought me here as a fun distraction. He was here on a mission.

Under the weight of my realization, the stakes suddenly felt incredibly high. As the noise in the room drowned out, the auctioneer announced the winner. I recognized him from my time in Paris with my father. The winning bid came from a notoriously cruel mafia boss known for his mistreatment of exotic animals.

I instinctively glanced at Lucien. The spark in his eyes burned brighter.

"He's buying it to hunt it down and turn it into a rug," Lucien hissed, his green eyes turning dark with determination. "How about you help me steal it?"

Hearing his words, my throat tightened.

"And if we got it, what would you do with it?" I asked, not sure where this was going.

He smirked, locking his gaze onto mine. "Who doesn't like rugs?"

I chuckled, unsure if he was serious. We had grown up mafia men, possessive and relentless. But there was always honor amongst the cruelty. So, was what my childhood friend had said a joke? Or was he introducing me to a side of him that I didn't want to know?

As much as I found his proposition absurd, there was a part of me that admired his audacity. More than that, there was a fire in his eyes that lured me from my drama-filled world.

"Alright then. I'm in," I said finally.

The surprise on Lucien's face was priceless. I wasn't sure what he was expecting me to say, but staring back at me, he beamed.

Reading everything Lucien's smile suggested, I thought again about what I had agreed to do. I was about to help my friend steal a tiger from a dangerous mob boss. Then, if we survived that, I had to convince him to give the beast to a zoo instead of hanging its head from his wall. None of this would be easy.

Listening to Lucien outline his plan, my heart thumped. This wasn't a joke he had come up with on the fly. He was deadly serious. Not only did he know the building's layout but he had memorized every door and alarm.

Had he worked here to gather intel? Because Lucien was prepared. And all I had to do was follow his lead and help push the cage when the time came.

Slipping into the warehouse's back corridors, Lucien's plan unfurled like a growing mist. We stealthily hugged walls and slipped beneath intricate alarms. Exiting a window, we threw ourselves onto a balcony that appeared too far away. Having lived a lifetime of heart-pounding moments, this had to top them all.

Back inside and drowning in adrenaline, Lucien's plan had worked. That is until a single misstep sounded an alarm. We froze, our heartbeats echoing into the vast looming dread. My mind spun in overdrive. Were we caught? The seconds ticked away into eternity before the alarm suddenly cut off.

Lucien breathed a sigh of relief, a half-smile playing on his face. I simply shook my head, my stomach clenching from tension. This recklessness, this wavering between life and death felt agonizingly familiar. And if I knew anything about times like these, I knew that the danger had only just begun.

It took only seconds to be proven right. As we descended the halls, a large man dressed in a cheap tuxedo turned the corner headed directly for us. He had come to investigate the alarm and as his jacket swished beside him, I saw that he was armed.

Before I could react, Lucien responded full of charm. Speaking in French, he weaved an elaborate story of paperwork mix-ups and absent delivery guys. He went as far as to produce an ID to prove his claims. It was an impressive performance.

The security man reassured yet annoyed that we hadn't followed the dress code, asked for my ID to confirm our story. Opening my mouth to speak, Lucien cut me off.

"Oh, he's my new guy. No ID for him yet. Fresh meat. Eager but doesn't know his left from his right."

His charm and glowing smile eventually disarmed the security man entirely. By the time Lucien was done with him, he was escorting us to the tiger. It took everything in me to not smile as I followed behind.

When more confusion arose standing in front of the man guarding the cage, Lucien handled that too. In the end, it was the security man who insisted the guard relinquish the tiger to us. It was a work of art.

Laughing as we wheeled the cage down the dim hallway, I said, "That was easier than getting into American clubs when we were kids."

"It helps when we both look like our balls have dropped," Lucien replied accusingly. "But don't jinx this, Remy. We're not done," he said, his focus unbroken.

"By the way, how do you plan to get this giant furball out of here? The Métro?"

He smirked and then pointed ahead of us towards a nondescript van in the parking lot.

"Great. Is that yours or are we stealing that too?" I asked confused.

Without a word, Lucien circled the van as we approached and popped open the back doors. Lowering metal slants, he stared at me waiting for me to do my part.

"So, you brought me as muscle?" I joked.

"I didn't bring you for your brains," Lucien quipped.

"Bastard."

"American."

"How dare you?" I demanded, my eyes squinting ready to fight.

Holding it for as long as I could, I quickly broke into laughter. This was our usual repartee. Its familiarity felt good amongst the absurdity of everything going on.

And I didn't just mean the tiger who eyed my hand on the cage like it was sausage.

Laughing with me, Lucien climbed down and helped me push the cage up into the van. As we drove away, my mind turned to the giant tiger in back. It was my turn to execute a mission. I had to convince him to give the animal to a zoo instead of whatever crazy thing he had planned.

I considered appealing to his pride and then his conscience. But before I could say a word, he pulled into an alleyway and cut the engine. As soon as things were quiet, a smaller African man approached the van.

"Lucien," he declared, "Where is he?"

"In back."

"Show me," the man insisted in an African accent.

I followed Lucien out of the van circling to the back. Popping open the doors, the agitated beast roared.

"It's beautiful. I promise it will live out the rest of its life on a preserve free from the cruelty of humans."

Lucien's eyes briefly met mine.

"Just keep your word. Don't make me have to come looking for you."

The small man looked up at my built cousin unintimidated.

"Don't worry. I will."

"Good," Lucien said before giving the man the van's keys and looking at me. "Let's go."

Catching up to him as he marched back up the alleyway, I stared at my childhood friend stunned. He was not the person I had once known.

"What?" He barked when he could no longer ignore my gaze.

"You softy," I teased.

"Are you talking about that? Were you expecting me to do the rug making myself? I don't get my hands dirty."

"Of course," I said seeing through him.

"Whatever," he said brushing my suggestion aside.

It felt like forever since the last time I had been surprised by life. I had grown up with Lucien. For a while, the two of us were practically one. He knew all of my secrets and I had known his. I had even told him that I had been with guys.

"Sometimes I like a change of scenery," I had told him playing it down.

"You're French," he had replied not batting an eye.

But that was then. Nothing I knew about him could have prepared me for tonight. Had he become some sort of vigilante for endangered animals? Considering the complexity of his plan, this couldn't have been his first heist.

Was this Lucien's true self? Was this what brought him his greatest joy? Maybe I had never known my cousin at all. Was that my fault? Was it also my fault that he didn't know me?

Weeks passed, and Dillon's continued absence seemed to etch itself deeper and deeper into my soul. Gone were the stolen moments, the gifts that made him smile, and the belief that we would eventually be together. All I was left with were the bitter reminders of what we had and could have been.

Eris, of course, was oblivious to how I felt. All she cared about was planning our wedding. She had to know it was all fake, didn't she? That I was only there to save the life of everyone I loved?

Maybe she realized it and was a better performer than even me. She had once said that she had as little choice in getting married as I did. But the way her eyes sparkled as she picked out place settings and center pieces made me wonder.

Sitting at my dining table next to Eris with our wedding planner shaping the sentence I would have to carry out, I again questioned every decision I had ever made. As I did, Eris reached across the table for my hand. Her fingers barely grazed mine before I snatched my hand back.

It hadn't been intentional. I had to be completely focused to get my body to act against what it wanted and today my mind was elsewhere. I had simply reacted.

Looking up at Eris, I caught the flicker of hurt in her eyes. Why? More than anyone, she knew that what we had was a lie. I was trying to make the best of things. I was trying to do what was right.

Couldn't she see the effort I was making? I was here, wasn't I? At no point had I killed or her father to get out of this. So what right did she have to act hurt by something I couldn't help?

Hours later when the wedding planning had mercifully ended, I found myself alone with Eris. We had been here before. I had never had to tell Eris to leave. She had always done it without asking. But there was something different about her tonight. This time as she sat staring at me, I saw a twinkle in her eyes.

"I want to do something for you," she said with a smile.

"Do you want to give me another watch?"

Eris's jaw tightened before relaxing. "No. This is better. You're going to like this."

"Am I?"

She shook her head before getting up. Looking for the remote control for the sound system, she turned it on. The music that played wasn't from any of my playlists. She had programmed it in. What was she doing?

As the slow sultry sounds poured from the speakers, she turned down the lights. She was setting the mood. For what? When she placed herself an arm's length in front of my chair, I found out.

Eris didn't have a bad body. Far from it. Her gentle curves, the subtle lines crisscrossing her stomach, she was every 14-year-old boy's dream. And the way she moved her hips to the music gave me thoughts. I couldn't help it. Even a gay man would appreciate what I was seeing.

Watching her, there was no question what she was doing. She had gotten tired of waiting for me to make a move so she was seducing me. Weirdly, it was kind of working.

In the time before Dillon had become my world, women like the one in front of me were my escape. In another time and place, Eris and I might have had a lot of fun together.

Reaching for my drink, I took another sip as Eris pulled her shirt over her head. She was wearing a bra that was barely there. God did she look good. Objectively speaking, the woman looked hot. I took another sip, and before I leaned forward and did something I would regret, I considered my drink.

How many had I had? I had certainly had one to help me get through the wedding planning, but how many after that? Was it just the one? I hadn't refilled my glass.

Thinking back on the night, I could remember Eris asking me if I needed another. I had reluctantly said yes. After that, there was never a time when my glass was half full. How many had I unknowingly drank, seven? Eight? How drunk was I?

I looked back at Eris who was now naked except for two pieces of shear cloth covering her nipples and swollen mounds. Yeah, she was fucking hot. There was no doubt about it. But did I want this?

Did I want this woman fucking me like her father had been doing for way too long? I didn't. So when she kneeled in front of me pawing my chest like a cat, I tensed. My hard cock might have given her the wrong impression, though. Rubbing against it and squeezing it, she got excited.

"Join me," she said standing and sashaying to my bedroom.

Not taking her eyes off of me, she removed what was left of her bra and dropped it. Yep, she had beautiful tits. And stepping out of what was left of her panties, she leaned against the door frame fully nude.

"You could have me whatever way you want," she said before disappearing within.

Did I want her? Did I want anything about her? What would my life be like if I just said yes?

Chapter 12

Dillon

Stairs creaked under my weight as I made my way down to Cali's kitsch-filled kitchen. The scent of bacon and waffles tugged me towards it. I could smell them from my bedroom.

Could you imagine my surprise when I walked in and found Hil at the stove? He was cooking everything by himself. Adjusting the bacon with one hand, he stacked a mountain of waffles with the other.

"Who would've thought?" I teased, trying to lighten my own mood as I strolled in. "Hil Lyon, mafia princeling turned master chef."

It was Cali who chuckled first. His shoulders shook as he poured coffee into a mismatched set of mugs. "You should've seen him when he first met."

"Oh, I can guess. Hil, have you told Cali about the time when I came over and you decided that you wanted scrambled eggs?"

"Oh god!" Hil moaned.

With Cali's full attention, I launched into the story.

"My mother was out shopping for something. I don't know what."

"She needed heavy cream to make my father's favorite tortellini." Hil looked up tickled by a thought. "And, I now know what all of those words mean."

"Tortellini?" Cali teased.

"Heavy cream. I remember her telling us that and me thinking, what does weight have to do with anything? Was it cream for cubby people?"

"Anyway," I interrupted. "Hil decided that he was going to make us eggs. So, he took two eggs out of the fridge and put them in the microwave because it was the only thing he knew how to do."

"Microwaves cook things and I wanted the eggs cooked. So I put them in the microwave," Hil explained to our laughter.

"Oh no," Cali exclaimed.

"Oh yes," I confirmed. "My mother had to then spend the rest of the day cleaning exploded eggs off of everything."

"She didn't make Hil clean it up?" Cali asked.

"The princeling?" I teased.

Hil looked away embarrassed. "I would have done it if I was asked. I felt bad."

"No, sweetie, my mother wanted it clean. If she had asked you, you would still be working on it today."

"And who would have made this amazing breakfast?" Cali inserted like a good boyfriend.

"I hate you both," Hil joked, tossing a dish towel at Cali.

I watched Hil and Cali's interaction. Envy twisted my gut. They laughed. They teased. They were happy.

I skimmed my fingers over the worn tabletop as my mind reverted to Remy, the cause of my grief. His absence echoed in the emptiness I felt. The weight of it drained me.

"I hate what he's done to you, Dillon," Hil muttered after a brief silence.

"Who?"

"You know who. Remy should've known better."

"I won't let you blame him, Hil," I replied, my words sharp – more so than I'd intended. At Hil's puzzled expression, I let out a sigh, running a hand through my loose curls.

"You warned me of exactly what would happen if I let myself fall for him. You told me and I chose to ignore it. So what happened is on me as much as Remy. If not more."

Playing with the silverware, I avoided the empathetic gaze of my two friends. Cali clapped his hands together, leveling me with a stern look. "No, Dillon. And I'm sorry to say this about your brother, Hil, but that man is a prick and an asshole."

"So, you're saying he can fuck himself?" I asked after some thought.

Cali froze thinking about what I had said before relaxing into laughter. Hil and I joined in.

"Yeah, he can fuck himself," Cali clarified.

"But, if I could do that, why would I leave my house?" A voice asked drawing our attention to the doorway.

"Remy?" I said immediately awash in all of my painful emotions.

Shooting across the kitchen and grabbing Remy's formal dress shirt in his fists, Cali was enraged.

"You have some nerve showing up here after the fucked-up shit you pulled," Cali snapped.

I hadn't seen him since leaving him standing naked in his bedroom in Paris. Yet there he stood framed by the morning sun. His broad shoulders filled the kitchen doorway, and despite the threatening grip Cali had on him, his dark eyes met mine.

He looked…wrecked like a storm had bruised his spirit. This was a far cry from his usual composed demeanor. Even his usually crisp shirt hung on him sloppily.

"Don't get your clodhoppers in a twist, hillbilly. I'm just here to talk to Dillon," he said lacking his usual fight.

"No," Hil spit, stepping in front of me as if to shield me from Remy's gaze. When Hil spoke again, his voice was bubbling with anger. "No, you have lost that right."

Hil's blatant refusal broke through Remy's façade. His typically controlled expression softened. Sadness flickered in his eyes. "Hil, you don't understand," Remy began, the roughness in his voice tugging at my heartstrings.

"What? That you did what you had to because Armand had not so subtly threatened to kill us all?" Hil said coldly.

"No, that I'm not our father," Remy corrected.

"What?" Hil asked thrown.

Remy sighed.

"Father would just settle something like this. He would have taken a few of his men and started a war that would leave a trail of blood in the streets," Remy said, his eyebrows furrowed.

"I know you think that's who I am, too. And maybe for a while, I believed it as well. But that's not me. I can't do that. I want to be able to protect the people I love like that, but I'm not him. I'm not Father."

With his admission, Cali let Remy go and backed off. Free, the two brothers stared at each other. I couldn't tell what either was thinking.

I knew what it meant to me. Remy was acknowledging what I always knew about him. He was a good man who had never wanted the life he was forced into.

"Remy, no one here wants you to be Father," Hil said breaking the silence as he clutched his big brother's shoulder.

"You have no idea how much I've sacrificed for this family, Hil. Yet, as much as I've thought about it, there's only one thing I regret."

"What's that?" I asked drawing his attention.

Remy left his brother to stand inches in front of me.

"I regret not telling you how I felt sooner," Remy declared raw with emotion.

My breath hitched.

"Dillon, I've been in love with you for so long. From the moment I met you, I could never get enough. Every time you came by to hang out with Hil, I wondered if you saw me. So, when I had you so close, when I had everything I ever wanted in my arms, I was the happiest I could ever be.

"When you left me, I tried living without you. I knew by doing it I would keep everyone here safe. But the request was too much. I can't stay away from you, Dillon. I need you. I'm here to tell you that if you'll have me, I will never leave you again."

I gathered my emotions, trying to reign in the overwhelming wave threatening to crash.

"Remy," I began softly, "I left you for a reason. You have to be with Eris. Everyone's life depends on it.

And even if it didn't, I can't be the other man. If I could, I'd do it for you. But I can't. I'm sorry!"

"But that's why I'm here," Remy explained. "I know I can't just walk away from Eris. But I also can't live without you," Remy declared baring his heart. "So I'm here to again ask for your help. I don't have all the answers like my father did. And I'm not him, I can't do this alone. I need the help of the people I love. And I love you."

Every word from Remy was like a balm to my aching soul. He loved me. Letting out a breath I didn't realize I'd been holding, I surrendered to him.

"I love you too, Remy," I confessed.

With that, Remy slipped his hand behind my neck and pulled me to him. Pleasure washed over me like a waterfall. His familiar lips were home. Feeling their warmth as he opened my mouth, I lost myself. And when his tongue entered in search of mine, I never wanted it to leave.

Electricity flowed through us. How did I think I could ever stay away from him? I couldn't. And as our two tongues danced and his other hand found my ass, the moment was shattered by my best friend reacting to seeing me kiss his brother for the first time.

"Should we leave?" Hil asked sincerely.

Nipping my lip as he pulled away, our two foreheads touched as we again found reality. Staring into each other's eyes, we giggled.

"Again, should we leave?"

"No, don't," Remy said straightening up. "I'm going to need your help as well." He turned from Hil to Cali. Yours too," He said vulnerably.

Cali stared at him.

"I still think you're an asshole," Cali concluded.

Remy chuckled. "It's my best quality," he joked.

"But, you helped me get Hil back," Cali conceded, his eyes softening. "So, I'll help you with this."

"We both will," Hil agreed. "It's time for the rest of us in this family to step up as well. It's not all up to you. We're in this together."

Relief washed over Remy. "Thank you. You don't know what this means to me. So, any bright ideas?"

I mulled it over, my mind racing with possibilities. "Do you think Armand has anything that could bring him down?"

"Don't we all?" Remy said with a smirk. Scanning our blank faces, he added, "Wrong crowd. Yes, there's a high chance Armand has something that could bring him down. What it could be and where we could find it, I have no clue."

"Don't all of you mob bosses follow the same playbook," Cali taunted.

"Sure, but I returned my copy of it to the library. If it wasn't for those darn late fees…," Remy replied sarcastically.

"Like I said, asshole," Cali concluded.

"And like I said, best quality," Remy teased returning to the man I loved.

"Seriously, do you think he has something we could use against him?" I repeated slowly forming an idea.

"Again, yes. But it's not like I shadow the man. It could be anything and anywhere. I wouldn't know where to begin."

"What if there's someone who would know?" I asked.

"Eris? There's no way she's gonna help me bring down her father. She's pretty pissed at me right now."

"What happened?" I asked unable to help myself.

"Let's just say that I left her at an inopportune time."

"Why?"

"Because when you realize you want to spend the rest of your life with someone, you want it to start immediately," Remy said gripping my soul.

"Cali, why don't you ever say things like that to me?" Hil asked his boyfriend.

Cali moaned and looked at Remy. "Asshole."

"Brother fucker," he said without missing a beat.

"Okay, you two," I said ending things before they started. "I'm thinking about Jimmy."

"The FBI agent?" Remy asked taken aback.

"You're friends with an FBI agent?" Hil asked confused.

"Oh, not just FBI. He's in the organized crime division," Remy explained happy to find someone who could relate.

"You're friends with an FBI agent who works in organized crime?" Hil said leaving Cali to question me.

"He's a friend from elementary school. We grew up in the same building. I ran into him when I was looking for a location for Remy's project," I tried to explain.

"And then he asked him to be on the board of the community center," Remy said enjoying this a little too much.

"You invited an FBI agent to be on the board of the community center?" Hil asked stunned.

"That's what I said!" Remy added gleefully.

"There are a lot of gangs in the area. He offered to help me make the center a safe space."

"You don't see how that could have been a questionable decision considering who was paying for everything?" Hil pushed.

"Not you too, Hil. Look, I did what I thought was best for everybody," I said starting to regret my decision. "If you want me to remove him from the board, I will."

Seeing me begin to sweat, Remy jumped in.

"No, no. I'm sure whatever decision you make is the right one. And they offer conjugal visits in prison, don't they? It's not like 10 to 20 years apart could break us up."

Cracking under the pressure, I squealed. "I'm sorry. I'll remove him immediately."

"We're teasing you," Remy explained with a smile. "Hil, tell Dillon you're just messing with him."

When Hil didn't respond, Remy said it again. "Hil, tell your best friend it was a joke."

"It was a joke," he said half-heartedly.

I looked at Remy whose eyes bounced between his brother and Cali.

"Okay people, I'm only going to say this one more time. I am not my father. I am a legitimate business person. Our family is now completely clean. There's nothing Dillon's FBI friend could get us on no matter how much Dillon wants him to."

"Remy?"

"Kidding!"

"Asshole!"

"Hillbilly."

Hil looked at us. "Now that we've gotten that part of the morning out of the way, what's next, Remy?"

"What do you mean?"

"You found Dillon. You've won him back. What now?"

"Come up with a plan, I guess," Remy said unsure.

"Well, you've said you need our help coming up with it. How about you stay here with us?"

"With us?" Cali quickly protested.

"Dillon's already here. He'll stay in his room." Hil turned to the two of us. "Right?"

I looked at Remy. "You're welcome to stay. It's going to take us a few days to flesh out a plan."

"You're suggesting I stay in Hicksville?"

"If he's going to disrespect our town like that..."

"I'm kidding. What is it about hill-folk that makes them unable to take a joke? Is it all the in breeding?"

Cali, charged towards Remy and grabbed his shirt. Remy allowed him with a smile.

"He's trying to get a rise out of you," Hil explained.

"It's working," Cali stated.

"Don't let it."

"And Remy, you said you need all of our help. That includes Cali. So, be nice!"

"Okay, fine. I'll be nice. I'm sure you have a lovely town filled with lovely people."

Cali's intensity melted eventually letting him go.

"And I'm sure only half of you share the same father," Remy added unable to help himself.

Cali's head snapped towards Remy but this time he didn't react. He just stared at him.

"Remy?" I chastised.

"Fine, a quarter of you."

"Remy!"

"There's only so much…"

"Remy, you need his help."

He sighed and gathered himself.

"This," he said gesturing to the bed 'n breakfast. "This is… lovely. Truly lovely. You should feel proud to have grown up in a place like this. Hil and I didn't and I'm sure we were made worse for it."

Remy turned to me.

"Are you happy?"

"I am," I said again surprised by his softer side.

"Thanks," Cali replied suddenly confused and disarmed. "You, ahh, want some breakfast? Your brother really knows his way around a kitchen."

"Does he?" Remy asked with shocked delight. "That's one of those things I'll need to see to believe," my guy said before sitting at the table and becoming a part of our group for the first time.

After we enjoyed Hil's impressive breakfast, Cali cleaned the dishes as the four of us brainstormed a plan. Remy described Hil's and my ideas as being ridiculously naïve, though he was sure to throw in a complement when it came from me. And my man described Cali's ideas as sociopathic, but to be fair, they were.

"We could just bomb the place and be done with it," Cali suggested while washing a plate.

"And that's an option," Remy replied before mouthing to me 'Is he serious?'

I looked at Hil for the answer. Hil's eyes bounced between the two of us with a look that said that he didn't know.

"That's what he did to us," Cali clarified. "Isn't that what people like him do?"

"Right. The bomb in the trunk thing," Remy said reminding us of what Armand's henchman did while trying to kill Hil. "So let's say we plant a bomb in his house and we kill him. We would have killed a man. You, with your small town 'Ah shucks', and please and thank yous, do you think you could live with that?"

"Why should we care what happens to him?" Cali asked bitterly.

"Okay," Remy said getting uncomfortable. "I know he shot you…"

"Yeah, he shot me," Cali said turning with venom.

"I know he shot you," Remy repeated trying to calm him down. "But, there would be no way you could live with yourself if you were a part of that. Yes, Armand is a piece of trash who doesn't deserve to live. But, you don't want to be the person who makes that happen. Trust me."

A knot in my stomach developed listening to Remy's plea. As it did, a heartbreaking truth dawned on me. It was the same for Hil and Cali.

"I've never killed anybody!" Remy shouted feeling everyone's stares. "Jesus! What do you all think of me?" he asked before getting up and storming outside.

I looked at Hil and Cali as they both looked back at me. Remy was right. We were all thinking it.

"I guess I should talk to him," Hil said apprehensively.

"No. I'll do it," I said hoping the time we spent together would make the conversation easier.

Exiting the kitchen and the bed and breakfast, I spotted Remy sitting in his car. I half expected him to drive off but he didn't. He just sat there behind the wheel. So I joined him.

"Having people think that was a lot easier when I didn't give a shit," Remy volunteered when my door was closed.

I shifted in the seat to face him and put a hand on his knee.

"What was it like growing up the way you did? It couldn't have been easy."

"Our father cared about his family. Never once did I question if he loved us. He said it constantly. But, my father wasn't a good man. I watched him do things to other people that he would burn in hell for if it existed."

"Like what?" I asked hesitantly.

"You don't wanna know."

"You're right. I don't. I would prefer to think of your father as the man who treated my mother well and paid for me to go to college. Never was your father anything but kind around me and I'd like to believe that that was who he was."

"And that's how you should remember him."

"No, it isn't."

"Why not? He's gone now. What does it matter?"

"It matters because you shouldn't have to carry the weight of what you've seen on your own."

Remy looked at me softening. "You couldn't take it. The things I've seen…"

"Ya know, I'm not as helpless as people think I am. I'm skinny, but I'm pretty strong."

Remy smiled. "I know you are. You're the strongest person I know. But you have your own shit to deal with. At least I had a father, as insane as he was. You had to raise yourself."

"I had my mother," I quickly added feeling defensive.

"Yeah, but you had no one to teach you how to be a man."

That quieted me. As a gay guy, growing up without a father was always a sore topic for me. When I was a kid and it became clear to everyone what I was, I overheard one of my mother's friends say that if she didn't bring a man into my life, I would turn gay.

My mother immediately came to my defense saying that there would be nothing wrong with if I did turn out gay. She said she would be proud of me either way. That shut her up.

But, hearing it as a kid, the idea that I was gay because I didn't have a father, lingered. It might even have been the reason I started watching my dad's family from across the street.

I have since learned that liking guys is more genetics than anything. And seeing how gay Hil is with a father like theirs, helped. But, the things you hear early are hard to shake. It sits in the back of my mind even today.

"You're right. I didn't have anyone to teach me what it was to be a man. But did learning what your father taught you make your life any better?"

Remy looked down in thought.

"Maybe not. Look, I didn't mean to say anything..."

"You didn't," I said knowing he hadn't. "I'm just trying to tell you that I want to be there for you. I want to help you carry whatever is weighing you down. I'm strong enough. I can take it. And I don't want you to feel alone. Not with me around," I said squeezing his knee.

Remy looked at me considering. When his decision was made, he said, "I once saw my father amputate a man."

"What do you mean?"

"I mean he started by cutting off each of his fingers with pruning shears before moving onto his limbs with a hand saw."

Shock and nausea flashed through me. "I don't understand. Why?"

"He had information that my father wanted and he wasn't giving it up."

"And he just cut off his limbs to get it?"

"And he made me watch," Remy admitted with pain in his eyes.

"What?"

"It wasn't just me. It was his whole crew. I think he wanted to show everyone what would happen if any of them ever betrayed him."

I had to steady myself as I digested the information.

"You okay there?" Remy asked this time touching my knee.

"Give me a second," I told him honestly.

He did and it was enough for me to start to process what I had heard.

"So, you see, when Hil or you think that I'm like my father, it means something a little different to me."

"I get that," I said compassionately. I paused. "I'm hoping that's the worst thing you watched your father do?"

Remy laughed. "How about we just leave it there for today? We're talking about a lifetime of stuff. I've had time to digest it. It might be a bit much to hear all at once."

"That's fair," I said relieved that I didn't have to hear more.

Remy turned and stared ahead at the colorful colonial-style building in front of us.

"What are you thinking about?" I asked scared of what I would hear.

"You were right. Telling you helped." He turned to me. "It's a lot, you know. But I feel a little lighter," he said with a smile.

"I'm glad," I said faking my enthusiasm.

"I shouldn't have told you, should I? I've traumatized you," he said with regret.

"No," I said before lowering my head knowing it was a lie. "I mean. Yeah, it's a lot. But that's what sharing the burden means. It means that no one person has to carry everything. We share the load. And, I'm strong enough. I can take it. Although, I might not be ready to go back inside just yet," I said forcing a smile.

Staring at me for a second, Remy turned and started the car.

"Where are we going?"

"I think we can take the rest of the day off. There were a few places around here I checked out when I was planning how to collect Hil."

"You mean when you were kidnapping him?"

"Potato, fries."

"Those are not the same thing."

"Eh," Remy said with a shrug before pulling off.

We drove for what felt like 30 minutes and eventually pulled over to the side of the street.

"Where are we?" I said looking through the windshield at a sea of trees in front of us.

"Did you know that there are more waterfalls in this area than anywhere in the country?"

I turned to Remy taken aback. "How do you know that?"

"I had to spend days here waiting for the best time to approach Hil. I had a lot of time on my hands."

"So you researched the town?"

"I did a Google search."

"And then what? You went hiking?"

"Your tone makes me think that you don't understand how much time I had to kill."

I leaned back in my seat and thought about it.

"So, after Hil caught you parked outside their place, you took off and did what?"

Remy thought about it. "I probably grabbed some breakfast at the diner. I might have done a hike I had marked on my hiking app."

"You have a hiking app?"

"I downloaded it when I was here. There are so many hikes here."

"So, let me get this straight. After making Hil think that someone was here to kill him, you would take a nature hike through the trails?"

"Firstly, there was someone here to kill him and it wasn't me. Secondly, you don't know how beautiful these trails are. I'm gonna show you. Come, let's go," he said patting my leg and then exiting the car.

Following Remy into the woods, I had to admit, he was right. I had resisted doing any of this when Hil had suggested it because, you know, bugs. But, I had never seen somewhere more beautiful in my life.

The lush trees that went on forever, the babbling stream that we crossed multiple times, they calmed me. And when after a mile we approached a pond fed by a waterfall, I was ready to sit and take it all in.

"I didn't know places like this existed," I admitted overwhelmed by everything.

"I thought the same thing."

"But you constantly make fun of Cali for being from here?"

"Oh, being from a beautiful place doesn't stop him from being a hillbilly. The two can both be true," Remy said with a devilish smile.

I didn't want to but I laughed.

"Cali's a good guy," I clarified.

"I know, I know. He's perfect. Never once did he watch his father dismember a person. I get. He's better than me."

"He's not better than you. He's just not as bad as you make him seem. You know he could end up being your brother-in-law, right?"

"And I'll be happy to have him. I will have to come up with a few more hillbilly jokes to add to the rotation. But it's what you do for family," he said with a smirk before unbuttoning his shirt.

"What are you doing?"

"You thought I brought you out here to show you the trees? We're here to get you naked," he said with a wicked grin.

I laughed unsure if he was serious. It turned out that he was. I watched Remy strip down to nothing and then dive headfirst into the water. I was shocked.

"Come in, the water's perfect."

I looked around at where we were wondering if Remy had lost his mind.

"Are you joking? We're in the middle of nowhere. We could be eaten by a bear or something."

"I think you skipped over the most important part of what you just said. We're in the middle of nowhere. There isn't anyone around for miles," he said wading in the water.

"Right, so there'll be no one around to hear me scream."

"Exactly. There's no one around to hear you scream," he said finally making his point.

My heart thumped staring back at the man I had desired my whole life. He was beautiful. With his sharp cheeks and chiseled jawline, it was like he was created from marble.

"Will you join me?" Remy asked suggestively.

"I shouldn't," I said feeling confused.

"But will you? I would like it so much if you did," he said seductively.

Remy's fiery eyes peered into me. It was like I was no longer in control. I needed to join him. I had to be close to him. So, standing and pulling off my clothes, I did.

"This water is not perfect. It's freezing!" I exclaimed when I surfaced.

"Then let me warm you up," Remy said pulling me to him.

Finding a place he could stand, Remy pulled me into his arms. His naked flesh pressed against mine. I could feel all of him, his built chest, his flat stomach, and his increasingly hard cock.

"I, ahh, don't want to give you the wrong idea," I told him slowly losing grip of my thoughts.

"And what idea is that?" he said with his lips close enough to my ear to feel his hot breath.

"That I want anything to happen between us."

"I would never do more than what you would want me to do. What do you want me to do, Dillon?" He asked sending chills down my spine.

In a flash, my cock became hard. Flinching against his stomach, he felt it.

"What do you want me to do, Dillon?"

If we weren't in cold water, I would have been sweating.

"I want you to…"

"To what?"

"Kiss me," I said shaking.

Pressing his cheek against mine, our chins touched. It was enough for him to move his lips closer to mine. Feeling his warm flesh push against me, I didn't react. I didn't know why, but I was feeling shy. It was like this was my first time. And without asking, he became my willing teacher.

Gently prying my lips apart, I felt his tongue touch mine. It made my brain sparkle. Brushing and pushing against it, it asked mine to join his. When the two of ours danced, his strength over me was evident. I was his to do with what he liked, and I wanted it all.

Losing myself in our kiss, I was reawakened to the feeling of his hard cock rubbing against mine. My dick wasn't small but the feeling of his length dwarfing mine further robbed me of my will.

His lower hand wrapped around my ass. His fingertip lightly touched my opening. He used it to guide my hips.

"What else do you want me to do?" He asked again whispering into my ear.

I didn't answer.

He ground his cock against mine filling me with thoughts.

"Tell me what you want," he insisted lowering my resistance.

"I want…"

"What do you want?"

"I want…" I began again instantly made drunk by the thought.

"Tell me," he demanded. "I want to hear you say it."

"I want you to fuck me," I said knowing it was true.

Immediately lifting me into his cradled arm, I held onto him. With my arms around his neck, my shyness was gone. As he walked us toward the waterfall, I kissed his lips. I didn't know where he was taking me, but as long as I was with him, I didn't care.

Entering the waterfall, the cascade enveloped us. The feeling was intense. My heart raced. As we stood there I could feel his tip penetrate my ass cheeks. It was looking for my hole and I wanted it to find it. When it did, I loosened my legs feeling his head pushing against me. It drove me wild.

Needing more, I rocked my hip trying to get him in me. All I felt was the pressure. Allowing my full weight to sit on his cock, I silently begged to feel him enter. He didn't. It was the water. The friction was too much.

It was then that, with my ass still cradled in his arm, we passed under the waterfall to its back side. The splash's echoes told me that we were in a cavern. The pond was shallower here.

Carrying me out of the water, Remy placed me on the soft ground of the shore. Not wanting to end our kiss, I held on as long as I could. It wasn't long. And with the circuit broken, he gripped the back of my knees and rolled my ass into the air.

The feeling of Remy's tongue on my hole was electric. I had never felt anything like it. If I hadn't already been, I would have gotten hard all over again. Squirming beneath his touch, my hole opened for him. And when the tip of his tongue tickled the inside of my opening, we both knew I was ready.

Gliding his body down mine, he placed my Achilles heel against his shoulder leaning down to kiss my lips. His tongue again entered my mouth. It was welcome.

As he parted my lips, his head touched my opening. Wrapping my tongue around his, my mind swirled as he thrust.

The ache washed through me. His size hurt until with a pop, he was inside of me. My insides gripped his cock.

Slowly easing himself into me, I froze feeling every inch of him. It felt so good that I could have cried. With his groin against my ass and his dick buried in my depths, he eased his way back. Not only was my man thick, but he was long. It took forever for his head to tease coming out.

But when it did, he repositioned himself on top of me and pushed back in. Remy was fucking me. I wasn't ready for it but I didn't want him to stop. He filled me completely. My eyes rolled back from the pleasure. And when he took my hard cock in his hand and stroked me to the rhythm of his fucking, I lost control.

"Ahhh," I groaned telling him I was close.

"Yeah," he moaned giving me permission to cum.

Fucking me harder, I bellowed. There was no one around so I could have. I let everything inside me out.

"Yes. Yes," I screamed.

"That's right. I wanna hear it."

"Fuck me. Fuck me harder."

Remy immediately obliged. I had never been fucked so hard in my life. If he wasn't pinning me down,

I would have slid away. And when the tingling ignited my body, it danced through me settling on my balls.

"I'm cumming, I'm cumming," I shouted as my toes curled almost breaking.

"Ahhhh," I yelled as my body clenched painfully and then released.

As I sprayed Remy's body with my juices, Remy filled my insides. It didn't take long for him to collapse on top of me. He was exhausted. So was I.

As much as feeling his body touch the sensitive skin of my cock sent me into a flurry of flinches, wrapping my arms around Remy made me relax. Everything felt so good that I could barely think straight. He was warm and comfortable and there was nowhere else in the world that I wanted to be. I never wanted this to end.

"I love you," Remy whispered into my ear.

"I love you too," I whispered back.

"I don't ever want to be away from you again," he said with heartbreaking emotion.

"You're the only guy I ever wanted," I told him knowing that I couldn't leave him again if I tried.

It felt like we had laid there together forever, but eventually, we had to get up. Knowing we had to wash off, we returned to the ice bath of a pond. Showering in the waterfall, I couldn't take my eyes off Remy. He had to be the most beautiful guy in the world and he was mine. I was willing to fight to the death to have him. Remy had become my everything.

Returning to the bed and breakfast hours after we had left, we found Cali and Hil on the back deck talking with two guys.

"These are my brothers, Titus and Claude," Cali told us to our surprise.

It wasn't that they didn't look like him. They did. It was more that Claude was black and he was darker than me.

Again looking for the family resemblance, it was unmistakable. When they smiled, their craterous dimples swallowed their face. God, were they hot. And if I understood their passing reference correctly, Titus was also dating a guy. Wow!

"I was thinking they could help us with that thing you were working on," Cali said to Remy's surprise.

"Why would you think that?" Remy replied employing the smile he used to mask his anger.

"They helped me keep Hil safe when…"

"When I came to get him?"

"When we were almost killed by a bomb," Cali said annoyed.

"Right. And I'm grateful for that. But I'm sure these fine gentlemen have better things to do than… help me move," Remy said talking in code.

"These are my brothers. If I asked them to "help you move," they will. And I would think that you would be grateful because we need the help."

"We don't need help."

"You think the four of us can handle that?" Cali said mocking Remy.

"Of course not," Remy said defensively. "That's why you hire professionals."

"Professionals to… help you move?"

"Yeah."

"You know professionals who could help you move?"

Remy was about to deploy his charm to dismiss the conversation when he froze. His charm was gone.

"I do," Remy said surprised.

He turned to me.

"I know someone who can help," he said glowing.

"You do? Who?" I asked not expecting what happened next.

Chapter 13

Remy

I strode through the community center doors, impressed by the buzz of activity inside. Kids dashed from room to room while volunteers tutored, cooked meals, and handed out donations. Dillon had created something incredible here.

My eyes scanned the crowd until they landed on him. Finding him, my heart skipped a beat. It was hard to believe that he was finally mine. The only thing still stopping us from fully being together was Armand and getting him out of the picture was what today was about.

"Hey you," Dillon said, approaching with a shy smile that made me melt.

"This place looks great. You've really built something special here," I told him sincerely.

Dillon's cheeks flushed at the compliment. "We both did. None of this would've happened without you either."

I started to protest but stopped myself. Dillon was right – my role in all this couldn't be denied. But his heart and vision were what brought this place to life.

"Is everyone here?" I asked, changing the subject.

He nodded. "Just about. They're waiting in my office. Be warned, Cali is a little more tense than usual."

"Okay, what did you say to him?" I joked.

"Nothing!" he declared with his gorgeous milk chocolate-colored eyes stripping me of my defenses.

"You didn't mention anything about dueling banjos, did you? Because I'm keeping that one on reserve for me."

"I don't know the reference," Dillon said looking at me confused.

"There's a scene in this classic movie called 'Deliverance' where two hillbillies kidnap this guy and tell him to squeal like a pig. Squeal like a pig! Squeal like a pig!" I recited in my best hillbilly accent.

"Remy, the only reason he's here is to help. Can you at least be nice to him until he's stopped risking his life for us?"

I lowered my head knowing the love of my life was right. "When it comes to Cali, I just can't help myself. He's so easy to make fun of."

"Try. For me. Please," Dillon asked, ensuring that I would.

"Anything for you," I told him before clutching his shoulders and kissing him. It had been too long since I had.

"Should we do this?" Dillon asked when I let him go.

"There's no time like the present," I told him before leading him to his office.

Entering, I looked around. Cali was pacing anxiously while Hil and Dillon's FBI friend, Jimmy, sat on the couch.

"Where's your professional friend?" Hil asked seeing me alone.

"Yeah. Where's this criminal mastermind you keep bragging about," Cali snapped.

My eyes darted towards Jimmy.

"Criminal mastermind at board games, you mean," I clarified.

"At board games?" Cali asked not understanding why I had said it.

"Yes. That's what I told you, remember. There's no one I know who can beat him at 'Clue'."

"What are you talking about?" He asked confused.

Jimmy cut Cali off. "Look, I don't care what games he's good at. The only question is, can he help us put Armand away?"

"Is that the FBI's official stance?" I asked tensely.

"Oh," Cali said before returning to pacing.

"All the Bureau cares about is putting New York's biggest crime boss behind bars."

Cali stopped staring silently at Jimmy.

I replied, "Good. Let's remember that," just in time for my ace in the hole to walk in.

"Sorry I'm late," a French accent said drawing our attention. "It was hard finding parking that didn't include me being murdered," he joked with a smile.

My fashionable cousin stepped in and looked around. "Ah, Americans", he said, immediately dismissing our motley crew.

"Who the hell is this?" Cali growled instantly hating everything about him.

I smirked. "The greatest game master you'll ever meet."

Lucien raised an eyebrow. "What is this, "game master?""

"Lucien, I would like you to meet Jimmy. He works with the FBI."

A flash of realization shot across my cousin's face. "Ah! Game master, like, how do you say, video games? Yes. Of course," he said shaking Jimmy's hand.

Jimmy looked at us unimpressed by our subterfuge. "Should we get on with this?"

"Yes, we should," Lucien said parking himself next to me. "What is it we are here to do, again?"

Jimmy looked at me annoyed. "He doesn't know?"

"Of course, he doesn't," Cali said returning to pacing even more tensely.

"He knows!" I clarified. "But, I'll say it again so we're all on the same page. We're here to steal books from Armand."

"Books?" Lucien asked confused.

"Accounting ledgers," Jimmy added. "An FBI source tells us that he keeps two sets of financial records. One is accurate. The other is for the IRS. If we can get a hold of both, we can put him away for tax evasion."

Hil chuckled. "After everything he's done, he's going to go down for tax evasion?"

"Unless you can find us a list of everyone he's killed and the murder weapons he's used, tax evasion is the only thing we've got," Jimmy told Hil.

"Then tax evasion it is," I said with a smile. "But, the problem is that we don't know where he keeps the ledgers."

"Actually, we know where he keeps them," Jimmy said correcting me. "They're in the safe of wherever he is. He's never away from them for longer than eight hours."

"Which helps us," I realized.

"If you consider them always being protected by armed guards helping us," Jimmy clarified.

"I remember them," Cali said subconsciously reaching for his bullet wound.

"We all do," Hil added.

Jimmy looked around confused.

"We've all had run-ins with Armand before," I told Jimmy.

"I see. And now you're marrying his daughter?"

"Not if I can help it," I told him taking Dillon's hand.

Jimmy's eyes darted to our interlocked fingers before bouncing back to my eyes in realization. Lucien's eyes did the same.

"I get it," Jimmy told Dillon as if he were putting things together.

"Yeah," Dillon confirmed.

"Okay then. What do we do?" Jimmy asked all of us.

We all looked at each other until our eyes stopped on Lucien who was lost in thought.

"Don't mind me. Continue on," Lucien said dismissively.

"Is there something you want to share with the group?" I asked my cousin apprehensively.

"About this? No. About planning my cousin's engagement party, maybe," he said with a smirk.

"Engagement party?"

"You don't think your best man would let this momentous occasion go by without throwing you an engagement party, did you?" He asked offended.

I was about to explain to him that I wasn't planning on getting married when he continued.

"The only problem is that I am visiting from France. For the number of people the bride's side of the family would want to invite, I could never find enough space. And then there's security. If only someone had a suitable location where we could throw a party," he concluded with a knowing smirk.

Jimmy stared at Lucien. "That might work," he said stunned.

"Brilliant!" I said starting to believe that we could do this.

"How do you say, "game master"?" Lucien joked.

"Whatever," Cali said finally relaxed enough to sit.

"I don't suppose you're going to tell me where you've been for the past week and a half," Eris asked me as we sat across from each other at Le Bernardin.

I picked up my drink and took a sip. "If only I had the time," I replied making sure she got the reference.

"I see you got rid of the watch."

"I didn't like the trace it left," I said touching my wrist.

Eris stared at me knowingly. "I could deny I know what you're talking about."

"You could but why insult either of our intelligence."

"It wasn't my idea," Eris said softly.

"Really?" I said doubtfully.

"Do you really think I know anything about putting a tracker in a transparent watch?"

"No. But I'm sure you could find someone who could figure it out."

Eris didn't respond. Looking away in guilt, she turned back more determined.

"Remy, why do we have to be on opposite sides?"

"Because what you want is not what I want, and you are a psychopath."

"I'm not," she said vulnerably.

"Which is definitely not what a psychopath would say," I said taking another sip.

"Look, Remy, I want to be married to you as much as you want to be married to me," she said dropping the façade.

"If that's the case, then let's call it off. Let's just walk away, forget this ever happened."

"So, what would you prefer, that my father kill everyone you know?"

"You're right. You're definitely not a psychopath. What was I thinking?"

"Am I wrong? Do you see any scenario where my father chooses to walk away from this while letting you keep your business or your life? Tell me, do you see that? Do you see anything like that happening?"

I thought about it. She was right and I knew it.

"That's what I thought. And do you see any scenario where I don't get married off to some asshole princeling that doesn't give two shits about me?"

I thought about that too.

"So, what I do, I do for survival. And I'm sorry that you happened to be the best of my truly awful options, but you are. So, you're going to learn to live with it, and you're going to do it without making me feel like shit for the rest of my life.

"I deserve happiness too, you know. And if you give us a real try, maybe it wouldn't be what either of us wants, but perhaps there's a way that we could still be happy," she said sincerely.

I lowered my head considering what she had said. She wasn't wrong. She was in as shitty a situation as I was. We were both trapped. There was no denying it.

I sighed in resignation.

"That's kind of why I brought us here."

"What?" Eris asked confused.

"You asked where I've been for the past few days. It was a place where I could get my thoughts straight. You're right. You've been right. Your father isn't going away. Like it or not, this is my new reality. Either I can accept it or die fighting it. And like you, I'm a survivor."

"So, what does this mean?" She asked apprehensively.

"It means, you win. I'm not going to fight it anymore. There's a path somewhere in there for me to be happy and I'm going to take it."

"You are?" She asked suspiciously.

"I am," I said resigned.

"That's good," Eris said doubtfully.

"It is what it is." I turned towards the door. "Oh. And on that note, there's someone I want you to meet."

I waved getting Lucien's attention.

"Who's that?"

"That's Lucien. He's going to be my best man."

Getting up as Lucien approached the table, I kissed him on either cheek and pointed him to a chair.

"Eris, this is my cousin, Lucien. Lucien, this is my fiancé, Eris." I said taking a seat.

Lucien looked at her like he had just seen Christ.

"Remy, you did not tell me how beautiful she is."

Eris, mesmerized by my charming cousin, melted in his gaze.

"He tends to forget that," she said offering him her hand.

Once he kissed it like she was the pope, I said, "Okay, well that's enough of that."

Lucien looked at me. "Do I sense a little jealousy?"

I turned to Eris. "Pay no attention to what he says. He's always had a thing for anything that belongs to me."

"Do I belong to you?" Eris asked intrigued.

"You will," I replied.

"I see," she said amused. "Last time I checked, I don't belong to anyone, and it is a pleasure to meet you, Lucien," she said with a smile.

"The pleasure is all mine."

"Okay!" I said breaking up whatever was going on.

"You are jealous! Who would have thought this was all it took?" Eris said with a chuckle.

"Yeah, well, like I said, I can see a path to happiness, and I'm willing to do what it takes to defend it."

"I like this new you," Eris said pleased. "And, if things don't work out between the two of us, maybe the three of us should give it a try."

"Enough!" I said fighting back my anger.

Eris laughed.

"Remy, relax," Lucien said. "I am just very happy to meet the woman my favorite cousin will be spending the rest of his life with."

"Yeah, I'm sure you are."

"I am," he said innocently.

"Anyway," I said changing the topic. "I invited Lucien here today because he had an idea."

"Yes," Lucien said taking over. "I was thinking, since Remy will only be getting married once, I would like to throw him a party."

"You mean a bachelor party?" Eris asked.

"Well, yes. But also something more formal. Something where our two families could get to know each other better."

"Like an engagement party?" Eris confirmed.

"Yes! How do you say? An engagement party."

Eris looked at me. "And you're okay with this?"

"This is not my idea."

Eris squinted as she stared at me.

"Do you think your family would come?"

"Do you mean considering your father shot my brother's boyfriend and then crashed my father's funeral?"

"What is this?" Lucien asked. "Crashed your father's…"

"It's nothing," Eris dismissed. "Water under the bridge. This is about starting our new lives together. A fresh start."

"Yes, a fresh start," Lucien said enthusiastically.

"What do you think, Remy? Would your family come?"

"Would we have a choice?"

"Of course. An engagement party would be about celebration. If you truly see a path to happiness, I think this is a step on it."

I considered what Eris said. "I'm not hosting an engagement party."

"You don't have to. We could rent somewhere," Eris suggested.

"Agh!" Lucien groaned. "You Americans are so impersonal."

"How about my father's place on Long Island? It's big yet personal. And you can walk out onto the beach."

"Ah, the beach," Lucien said intrigued. "This sounds good, no?"

I hesitated. "I don't know if I would be up for this. A lot has gone down between our two families."

"That's an even better reason to do it. Please, Remy, I have looked past a lot of stuff and you know it. I deserve this. Give this to me."

I looked at Eris with sincerity. "You're right, you deserve this. I'll talk to my family. Everyone will be there."

"Oh Remy, thank you," she said clutching my hand from across the table. "I'm so excited."

"Me too," I told her before turning to Lucien who greeted me with a wink.

When dinner was done I told Eris that I was going to spend some time with Lucien since I was the reason he was in town and he didn't know anyone else here. As far as I could tell, she bought the excuse so it became my go-to for whenever we needed to get together to go over plans.

"Remind me again how we're gonna get into the safe," Cali demanded as tense as ever.

"Remind me if getting into the safe is your job," I retorted.

"No, but…"

"Then why don't you just focus on your part of the plan and not screw that up," I shot back quieting him.

"Fine, then how about you remind me," Jimmy said standing up threateningly. "Considering the FBI is funding this little venture, I think the Bureau has a right to know."

My eyes darted between Cali and Jimmy who now stood together against me. A part of me wanted to tell the both of them to fuck off but I had to admit that Jimmy's toys were fun.

"Let's just say that the work I did for my father required unique skills."

"So, you're going to crack the safe," Jimmy asked bluntly.

Not fully trusting Jimmy, I wasn't about to answer that. "If I encounter a safe, it won't stop me from getting what I want."

Jimmy's eyebrow raised suspiciously. "Should we make a contingency plan for any type of explosion?"

"Only if we also plan on hiding C4 in the cake. Will we be storing C4 in the cake?"

Jimmy looked at Cali, Hil, and Lucien. "Are we?"

"No!" I replied annoyed. "Don't you think that would have been something that we would have discussed before now? Do you think baking a cake with C4 in it is something one pulls out of their ass two days before the job?"

"Remy, can I talk to you outside?" Dillon said grabbing my attention.

I turned back to Jimmy much preferring to continue making him look stupid, but I had a hard time not giving Dillon what he wanted.

"Sure," I said giving Jimmy the side eye.

Following Dillon out of his office and onto the street, he waited for the door to close before turning to me.

"Remy, what were you doing in there?"

"You heard me. I was answering a bunch of stupid questions."

"No, you weren't. You were attacking the people who are only here to help us have a life together."

"Dillon, they're treating me like I don't know what I'm doing."

Dillon shook his head with sadness in his eyes. "Remy, they're treating you like they don't know what they're doing. And they don't. The most Cali's ever done is help you rescue Hil when Armand kidnapped him. And until now, Jimmy has only done desk work. You have to keep that in mind when you talk to them."

"Yeah, but…"

"No "buts". I know you and Lucien have had a life full of this stuff. But no one else here has. You have to take that into account. We're all scared shitless that something will go wrong. Armand's already shot Cali once. We know what he's capable of. Help us have your confidence in the plan," Dillon pleaded with his soft brown eyes wide.

Staring down at the man I loved, I realized that I had a problem. For the rest of our lives together, I would never be able to say no to him. He had me wrapped around his little finger.

"You're right. I'll do what I can. Are we good?" I asked affectionately squeezing his shoulders.

"Always," he replied looking up with a twinkle in his eyes.

Kissing him under the street lights, I remembered how lucky I was to have a man like Dillon by my side. He was everything I wasn't. He helped me be the person I always wished I was.

Heading back into the center and the office, I addressed everyone.

"Okay, we'll go over this again. And we'll keep going over it until everyone here is comfortable with what they have to do," I said looking back at Dillon.

The smile he gave me in reply melted my heart.

"Tomorrow I'll suggest to Eris that she and I spend the night at Armand's place so we don't have to deal with Saturday afternoon traffic into Long Island. Knowing her father won't be there, she'll have no reason not to agree. Once there, and I'm sure Eris is asleep, I'll use this handy toy," I said holding up the glorified stud detector that Jimmy supplied from the FBI.

"With it, I'll search the walls of Armand's bedroom and office for his metal safe which this should detect easily. Once I've found it, I'll crack it."

"But, the ledgers won't be in it yet," Jimmy pointed out.

"The house will also not be swarming with security. That way, if it takes me a little longer to figure out the combination, no problem."

"Right," Jimmy agreed.

"And once I have it, I head to bed. In the morning, I have breakfast with Eris and I wait for the catering to arrive."

"That's when I get there," Dillon interjected.

"Yes. Because if Armand's security team is worth their salt, before anyone arrives, they are going to do a bug sweep. They can't do it once catering and the planners start setting everything up. It will be too busy.

Which means you, Dillon, can get there as part of the party planner crew and plant the bugs and repeaters we'll need to communicate with Jimmy's van which will be parked a quarter mile away."

"I'm still not comfortable with not being able to come in and help you if something goes wrong," Jimmy added.

"What could you do? Run in guns blazing? You'd shot dead as soon as you stepped onto the lawn and Armand would get off with a slap on the wrist for defending his property."

Jimmy's jaw clenched.

I looked back at Dillon hearing his voice in my head. He didn't have to say anything to get me to approach Jimmy with a hand on his shoulder.

"Look, we're gonna be okay. As long as everyone does what they supposed to, we'll all be in and out before Armand knows anything's missing. After that, your people will examine the ledger to determine its legitimacy. Once that's done, Armand gets arrested and the FBI convinces him not to retaliate on any of us," I said clenching my jaw in doubt.

"I told you, this isn't the FBI's first mafia boss. We know what we're doing. He won't be stupid enough to come after you once we're done with him."

"I hope so," I replied still not trusting him.

Repeating the details of the plan until everyone was comfortable with it, I said good night and left with Lucien.

"You know, he's good for you," Lucien said as we drove back to my place.

"Dillon?"

"Yes, Dillon," he said amused. "He mellows you out."

"You think I need mellowing?"

"You have been known to be a little intense. Very single-minded. Not much thought."

"I see. Care to mention anything else that's wrong with me."

"You're defensive?" He said teasingly.

I laughed.

"If you knew what I've seen… the things I've done," I said with a huff.

"We've all seen things. We've all done things that we didn't want to and now have to find a way to live with. But that one, he calms your waters."

"He does," I admitted.

"You love him?" He asked getting more personal than he had in a long time.

"I do."

"It shows," Lucien said with a smile. "It's a good thing."

"It is," I replied knowing how lucky I am.

"Now, about this plan. Do you really think this group will pull it off? I mean, Dillon is great for you but can he plant the bugs."

"Dillon will be fine."

"And the big guy who always looks like he's about to lose his shit, can you trust that he'll be able to do what he has to when the time comes?"

"Let me tell you something about him. There's no one in that room that I trust more."

"I was in that room."

"But you've never taken a bullet for me."

Lucien's mouth dropped open. "Remy, I love you, but…"

"Don't worry. I feel the same," I said snidely. "But that one, Cali, he's the type you go into battle with."

"And you're sure about that?"

"I'd bet my life on it."

"And you're going to," Lucien reminded me. "You're betting your life on all of them."

"My life has never been in better hands," I said turning to him with a smile.

"Must be nice," Lucien said turning his gaze to the windshield.

"It is," I told him before we both fell into silence.

The next day after convincing Eris that we should stay at the beach house the following night. I checked in with the team one more time before I left.

"You can do this, Dillon. You all can," I told him over the phone as I drove to pick up Eris.

"This is it, isn't it? Either we pull this off or…"

"There's no "or". We're going to do this. And once it's done, we'll be together."

"I love you, Remy. I need you to know that."

"I love you too, Dillon. I've always loved you and I always will," I told him knowing it was true.

Pulling up to Eris's place I knew the game had begun.

"Hello," she said going in for a kiss.

My instinct was to turn away but I didn't. I let her kiss my lips. Everything had to go perfectly tonight. We couldn't get into a fight. That meant doing more than I was comfort with.

"We're going for the weekend," I reminded her as I stared at the two suitcases she needed me to carry down three flights of stairs.

"That's why I packed light," she said without a hint of irony.

With the car loaded and us on our way, I again went over the plan in my head. There couldn't be any mistakes. There was no margin for error.

I wasn't sure what Armand would do if he caught us, but he wouldn't just let it go. He would make an example of someone. And if he was anything like my father, the example would suffer.

Having second thoughts as I pulled into Armand's driveway, my resolve returned when Eris exited the car without a thought to her stuff. She expected me to bring it in for her, which I would. But could I stand to play the role of thankless husband to a spoilt rich girl for the rest of my life? Not when I had Dillon waiting for me.

"I'll put them over here," I said depositing her suitcases outside our closet.

"If that's what you want," she said posing seductively on the bed we would share.

I looked at her knowing what was soon to follow. I had avoided having sex with her so far, but my excuses were wearing thin.

"Did you say that the chef left dinner for us?"

"Yes. She said that all we needed was to warm it up," she said wiggling her chest and lightly biting her finger.

"Well, I'm starved. Did you want me to warm you up some, too?"

"Ahh. Fine!" She said giving up and flopping onto the bed.

Leaving her, I headed downstairs to the kitchen and went to work. I knew what the chef had prepared for Eris because it was the same thing she ate every night, a kale salad topped with a grilled chicken breast and mixed fruit for desert.

Opening the fridge, that was what I found. Retrieving the items and placing them on the kitchen island, I looked behind me and pulled a vile from my pocket. Pouring the contents over the fruit in both bowls, I quickly mixed the concoction and returned the empty vile to my pocket.

"What did the chef make us?" Eris said entering the kitchen behind me.

"Guess," I said sure that she had requested it.

She looked over everything laid out in front of us.

"I'm sure she made you a pan of lasagna or something. Check in the fridge."

"I did," I said knowing that the chef would have if Eris had asked.

"Oh well. This is better for you anyway," she said grabbing a bottle of wine and glasses.

"I'm sure," I replied knowing I could never take a lifetime of this.

Watching her eat, I tried not to stare. When she was done with the salad, she moved on to the fruit.

"The fruit is really sweet," she said staring into the bowl. "It's good. I like it."

"Me too," I said eating my portion after her.

With the wine flowing freely, Eris turned to me with a telling look in her eyes.

"Do you think I'm pretty?"

I looked at her. There was no question that she was.

"You're one of the prettiest women I've ever met," I said honestly.

"Then why don't you want to have sex with me? Is it because you're gay?"

"And if I was?" I asked fantasizing about finding a way out.

Eris laughed. "I've heard stories. I know you're not gay. But what is it?" She said feeling the alcohol.

"Maybe I was just waiting for the right time," I suggested suddenly filling her with hope.

"And what time is that?"

"Maybe it was the night before our engagement party at a beach house we had to ourselves."

"Oh yeah," she said excitedly.

"Yeah," I replied with a smile.

"Would you like to kiss me?" She asked with drunken apprehension.

"Maybe I would," I said staring at her.

"Then, why don't you do it?" She asked shyly.

"Then, why don't you come here."

Eris got up from her stool across the kitchen's island and immediately bent forward.

"What's the matter?" I asked innocently.

"Nothing, it's just my stomach," she said before straightening up and trying again. "Oh," she said pausing. "Excuse me."

Erythritol is a zero-calorie sugar alcohol put in deserts to lower its calorie count. A few months ago she had tried a new brand of protein bar that didn't agree with her stomach. The main ingredient? Erythritol, which is also available in granular form in the baking aisle.

"What's the matter, dear? Not feeling well?" I yelled while cleaning up the dishes.

"I'm fine. I'll meet you in the bedroom," she yelled back.

"I'm sure you will," I muttered under my breath.

Lying in bed with my shirt off, I waited for my fiancé. When she arrived, she didn't look as confident as she usually did.

"I don't feel well," she said keeping her distance.

"What is it? Is it your stomach?" I asked caringly.

"Yeah."

"Is it gas?"

"I don't get gas," she said defensively.

"Then what is it?"

"It's nothing."

I smiled seductively. "Then, why don't you join me?"

She took a step toward me and farted. "Oh!" It was so adorable that I almost mistook her for human. Quickly backing off, she said, "Not tonight."

"What do you mean "Not tonight"?"

"Just, not tonight."

"But I had all these plans about what I was going to do to you."

"Not tonight!"

"Okay," I said disappointedly. "Would you prefer I let you have the bedroom? There are other rooms I can sleep in."

"Yeah, do that."

"I mean, if you insist," I told her collecting my bag and exiting the room.

As soon as I was in the hallway, the bedroom door slammed behind me with a crash. It was followed by the longest fart I had ever heard. In a few hours, she would be fine. That meant I had until then to find what I was looking for and do what I had to do.

Parking my stuff in the 3rd bedroom, I retrieved my safe finder and went to work. The process was tedious but I did it. Starting with the master bedroom, I searched every inch of the wall. When I was done there, I checked the master bath.

I knew the chances of the safe being in either of those places were low, but this was the best time to do it, while the effects of the erythritol were at its peak. What excuse could I give Eris if she caught me in Armand's bedroom, especially since I had to pick the lock to get in?

Luckily, I didn't have to give any. And if she walked in on me in Armand's office, I could always say that I was looking for a book to help me fall asleep. It wasn't a great excuse but it would work.

Opening Armand's second-floor office door, I slipped in and locked it behind me. Alone, I examined the space.

The first places I checked were the pictures on the wall. Jimmy's device said there was nothing behind them. I next checked the wall-length bookshelf. Nothing there. Sitting at his desk chair, I checked his desk. Still nothing.

I was about to declare that Jimmy's device didn't work when I noticed something. The office had two air vents. One neared the ceiling. The other neared the floor.

On its own, this meant nothing. Ceiling vents are better for cooling while floor vents are better for heating. I probably wouldn't even have noticed it if I hadn't just finished scanning every inch of the bedroom.

Putting the safe finder next to the floor vent, it immediately went off.

"Gotcha," I said freeing my hands and prying open the vent.

Behind it was a standard consumer-grade wall safe. I recognized the brand. It had cost me a lot of money to get the retrieval code for it a few years back. I had my father to thank for that. One day out of the blue my father told me it was time for me to learn to crack a safe. It was a skill he had and I was expected to have it as well.

The problem was that I turned out to be horrible at it. I suspected that it had to do with the added technology since my father's day, but he refused to acknowledge the change. When I brought it up, he said I was making excuses. So, instead of continuously bashing my head against the wall, I did what any smart person would do, I bought the company that built the safe.

It was my first legitimate purchase. Buying it was what started me on my new path. From them, I learned that every safe company incorporates backdoor codes that can open any of their safes. They call it a failsafe in case of emergency. But for the right price, it can be yours.

The only problem with the brand of safe in front of me now is that their failsafe is 16 digits long. And to ensure their safes aren't easily compromised, they include 49 dummy combinations with the one that works. It was looking like a long night, and it was.

"Finally!" I said three hours later when I identified the correct combination.

Opening the safe I found it to be empty except for about $50,000. That surprised me. Growing up, my family's penthouse had been exploding with cash. My father couldn't launder the money fast enough. What did Armand do differently that left only petty cash in his safe?

Putting that mystery aside, I made note of the safe's combination and closed it. Returning everything to how it was when I had entered, I re-locked the office and headed for my room.

Lying in bed I thought about everything going on. It was all dependent on Jimmy being correct about Armand carrying his ledgers with him. If he was wrong, we were all screwed. How had I gotten here?

For so long I had lived life like I had no future. I had accepted that I was my father's son destined to follow in his bloody footsteps. But then a miracle happened, Father got sick. As tragic as it was, it was the first time I pictured a way out.

It was then that Dillon had become my motivation. Having not crossed any lines, I could still become a man he could love. It was because of him that I came up with my plan to go legitimate. And I was about to get everything I ever wanted until Armand interrupted my father's funeral. He couldn't just be satisfied with my father's empire. He had to have mine too.

That would be his downfall. Because what he didn't take into account was who I would become with Dillon by my side. Dillon was more than my inspiration. He was my guiding light. I didn't know who my true self was until Dillon made me think about it.

Yes, 'Embrace your true self and you will be rewarded' had been my father's saying, but it's hard to see yourself without a mirror. Seeing myself through Dillon's eyes was the mirror I needed.

I wasn't who I thought I was. I was someone who felt more than just lust. I was a person who needed more than to keep my loved ones safe.

Those things were a part of me, of course. But it wasn't all I was. Dillon helped me see that. And once I had, for the first time in my life, I understood that I wasn't my father. I was just his son.

Growing up with my father had shaped me. But it hadn't turned me into someone else. I could still be kind and less guarded. I could still be a guy Dillon could love.

Forcing my thoughts aside, I went over the plan one last time and then rolled over to go to sleep. When I woke up the next morning, the sun was still rising. I couldn't have slept more than four hours and I felt like it. My brain was working slower than usual. And considering it was the one tool I needed to survive today, this wasn't good.

I tried to catch a few more winks but as soon as I closed my eyes, the plan spiraled through my mind. Would Dillon be able to keep out of sight while planting the bugs? Will Cali hold himself together when he looks into the eyes of the man who shot him and kidnapped Hil?

Past that, I had to get in and out of Armand's office. His security team would be everywhere. This had been Lucien's plan and my cousin was certainly a genius. But in the light of day and with my brain working at half capacity, this was feeling impossible. Did I call it off before someone I loved got hurt?

A soft knock on my bedroom interrupted my thoughts.

"Yes?" I asked wondering if the house staff had arrived early.

Eris took that as her invitation to enter. Dressed in a sheer nightie that showed off more than her perfect body, she crossed the room and climbed into bed with me. Making herself my little spoon, she wrapped my arm around her slender frame.

As soon as she did, I tensed. I hated that it was her body pressed against me instead of Dillon's. But we lay together in silence until my tension caused her to whisper, "Do you really want to go through with this?"

She meant our engagement party. But it was the question I was asking myself about the heist. Feeling her body where Dillon's should have been, answered my question. And knowing that this could be how it was for the rest of my life, made me sure.

"Yes, I truly do," I answered, hoping she couldn't detect the edge in my voice.

Eris smiled, seeming pleased with my response.

The longer I lay next to her, the more reinvigorated I felt. Refocused, I then ticked off each part of the plan as it occurred.

Right on time, Armand's security team arrived. Hearing them shuffling around downstairs, Eris and I got dressed and headed to the kitchen. Grabbing cups of coffee, we drank it on the back patio.

It took security over an hour to go through every room. As they did, I watched them thoroughly while Eris lost herself in the view of the pool and beach beyond it.

When the suited men found no hidden cameras or mics, they gathered for a quick meeting and then left. That was when the kitchen staff and caterers arrived. Discussing logistics, they searched the space as intently as Armand's security had. On the heels of that, the event planners and their crew arrived.

As soon as I saw Dillon in his meager disguise, my heart thumped. It wasn't going to be enough if Eris spotted him. There was something too recognizable about the way Dillon moved.

"I just had an idea," I said drawing Eris's attention.

"What's that?"

"It's our engagement party, isn't it?"

"Last time I checked," Eris snipped.

"We should coordinate what we wear."

It surprised me how much Eris's face lit up. "Really?"

"We're a couple, aren't we?"

"Yeah," Eris said delighted. "See, that's why I brought two suitcases."

"It makes sense. Good thinking ahead," I said with a smile.

Eris couldn't be more pleased with herself.

"Should we compare what we've brought?" I asked.

"Now?"

"Why not?"

"Okay, let's go," she said happily.

"Lead the way," I said prompting her to get up.

When she had turned facing the other way, I looked back a Dillon. I was worried for him. What if Eris had mentioned him to Armand and Armand arrived early knowing what Dillon looked like?

Putting him in this type of danger was a mistake. Nothing was worth risking his safety, but there wasn't anything I could do about it now.

Eris's parade of dress options seemed endless. That was good because it kept her in our room where she was sure not to spot Dillon. But, seriously, how many dresses could one woman own?

When I couldn't take anymore and I was sure Dillon was safely gone, I suggested what we should wear and brought the nightmare to an end.

"Okay, give me some time to get dressed."

"I thought you were dressed," I said sincerely.

Eris looked at me like I was a naïve child. "It's our engagement party. I need to put my face on silly."

"Right. Well, I'll see you out there."

"Not if I see you first," she said as she disappeared into the bathroom.

Getting dressed and running my fingers through my hair, I took a quick look in the mirror and left the room. I was feeling confident. Heading downstairs about to check in with the kitchen, I saw two things I didn't want to.

Through the open front door, I saw Armand pull up. And through the glass door leading to the back patio, I saw Dillon desperately trying to get my attention. When he had it, he beckoned me outside.

"You're supposed to be gone by now," I told him pulling him to a secluded section of the backyard.

"I know. I know," Dillon said panicked.

"Okay, Dillon, calm down. Tell me what's going on."

"It's the equipment. It's not working. I did everything Jimmy told me to do when I planted them, but he's not getting a signal."

"Fuck!" I muttered trying to figure out what to do.

My heart was thumping. Jimmy's recording was our back up plan. If everything went to hell, he would hear and call in the cavalry, whatever good that would do. It was also a second option in case I couldn't get a hold of the ledgers. I was supposed to pull Armand to where I knew a bug was planted and discuss business. Without the recording, not only did we have one shot at this, but if anything went wrong, we were on our own.

"Jimmy thinks Armand's men put in something that can scramble a radio signal."

"I've never even heard of such a thing," I told him.

"Neither had I. But Jimmy says they exist. Who's that?"

"Who?" I asked lost in thought.

"Up there?"

I turned to Dillon and followed his gaze. Looking behind me I saw a face in the second floor window. The person was staring down at us until they quickly pulled away. Counting the windows, I knew exactly who it was.

"Shit!"

"Who was it?" Dillon asked scared.

"Eris. You need to get out of here fast."

"What about the recording?"

"We won't need it. I'll get the ledgers and we'll be fine."

"Are you sure?"

"Yes. Go. And on the way out, retrieve as many of the bugs you've planted as you can. We don't want anyone stumbling on something by mistake and blowing everything."

"Okay."

"And, Dillon, once you're out of here, I want you as far from this place as possible. Make it somewhere where no one can find you, not even me."

"Why?" He asked with fear in his eyes.

"Just do it. I'll contact you as soon as I can. But if you don't hear from me, I want you to disappear and not look back."

"Remy?" He said terrified.

"Please, Dillon. I love you. And I need you to go."

He stared at me not wanting to leave. I wanted to kiss him. It took everything in me not to, but I knew I couldn't. Too many things had already gone wrong.

Letting Dillon go, he pulled his cap further down his forehead and snatched devices out of planters as he left. Was this the last image I would ever see of him? I couldn't think about this now. The only important thing was that he got out of here safely.

Heading back inside and into the living room, I saw that Armand wasn't the only person to arrive. Talking to him in an animated conversation was Lucien. I could only imagine what they were discussing. Needing to keep Armand distracted while Dillon escaped, I headed over.

"Your soon-to-be stepfather," Lucien said with excitement as I approached.

"Yes, we've met. Lucien, this is Armand." I turned to Armand. "Lucien is my cousin from the French side of my family."

"And his best man," Lucien added enthusiastically.

"The French side of your family?" Armand asked looking at Lucien knowingly. "I've heard things."

"All good I hope," Lucien replied. "Were you friends with Remy's father?"

Armand looked at me and smiled. "We were respected colleagues," he said smugly.

"Ah," Lucien said before pausing. "Ahhh!" He repeated as if suddenly getting his meaning. "So, you're marrying into the family business," Lucien said to me with a hand on my shoulder and a pat on my stomach. "Good man! Good man."

"And you two are related how?" Armand asked Lucien.

As Lucien explained, I looked up to see Dillon snake his way up to the event planner's van and then past it into the street. I was sure that there would be security on the feeder road leading here. But they were there to prevent people from getting in, not out.

With Dillon now safe, I turned my attention to the other part of our plan. Lucien had to have caught Armand on the way in because under his arm was a leather satchel. It had to be where he kept the ledgers.

"Lucien, can I talk to you for a moment?" I asked interrupting their conversation. I turned to Armand. "It's best man stuff."

"Of course," Armand said turning to the stairs. "It was a pleasure to meet you. We'll talk more. Perhaps there are ways our two enterprises could work together."

"Intriguing prospect," Lucien said with a smile. "I'll find you later," he told Armand as he ascended the stairs. "That was interesting," Lucien muttered when Armand was gone.

"You two seemed to get along," I said unimpressed.

"I've had a lot of practice dealing with men like him. It's not hard to figure out what types like his want to hear."

"Well, you're not gonna want to hear this. Not only has Armand's men turned on something that's blocking the radio signal of our bugs, but I'm pretty sure Eris saw me talking to Dillon."

"Shit!"

"Shit is right."

"What are we going to do?"

"Aren't you the mastermind?" I asked sarcastically.

"Didn't you hear? It's in video games not complete shit shows like this."

I chuckled feeling screwed. "Do we call it off?"

"Give up? What are you insane? This shit show hasn't even begun."

I laughed. "I just needed to hear you say it."

"It is said. Now we dance."

"What?"

Lucien shuffled his feet looking at me.

"Oh, tap dance!"

"Yes, this. We tap dance."

I looked at him with a smile. "Then here goes nothing."

"Here goes," he told me before leaving me to greet a guest I had never met.

It didn't take long for the open-layout living room to fill with people I didn't know. It was a relief when I saw a few friendly faces. And before I could cross the room to talk to them, Cali had already started his second drink.

"Maybe you want to slow down there, Champ," I said staring intensely at Cali.

"Don't call me Champ," he replied with a feistiness he had never had.

"Okay," I said looking at Hil worried.

My brother shrugged apologetically.

"And how are you, Mother?" I asked kissing her on the cheek.

"I'm here. That has to be enough," she said sternly.

"I get it," I said taking the drink out of Cali's hand and drinking it.

"Hey!" he said annoyed, before leaving us to get himself another.

"I don't think you should push him today," Hil told me, his brows furrowed.

"Or maybe you should keep your hillbilly boyfriend on a shorter leash."

"Remy!" My mother rebuked.

"Relax, Mother. Hil knows I'm just joking around. Today is difficult enough without being able to blow off a little steam."

Hil leaned towards me. "I'm just saying, he isn't in the best state of mind right now."

"Who is, little bro? Who is?" I asked leaving the pair behind.

With Armand back at the party circulating with the guests, I began looking for openings to leave. But what became more and more disturbing was that my fiancé had yet to make her appearance. This couldn't be good. There was no denying how much Eris liked making an entrance, but it had been over an hour since she saw me talking to Dillon. I had to believe that her absence wasn't a coincidence.

"So, where is my daughter?" Armand asked me when he found me alone.

I stared into his eyes needing to figure out what he knew. Had Eris told him what she had seen? Were there already men looking for Dillon to end his life? I was about to call the whole plan off when down the stairs walked a sight for sore eyes.

"She's right there," I told Armand turning his attention to Eris.

When everyone's attention had turned, I clapped drawing everyone's applause. Eris stopped, blushed, and waved to everyone.

"My fiancé," she said gesturing towards me.

When everyone's eyes were on me, I approached the stairs and took Eris's hand. The crowd continued to applaud. The only one who wasn't was Cali.

How many drinks had he had at this point? I had lost count at five. This was not good, but I could only deal with one problem at a time.

Holding Eris's hand, I led her into the crowd. Looking back at her, she refused to look at me. Yep, she had recognized Dillon. There was no doubt about it. The only question now was when this powder keg was going to explode.

Engaging with a mixture of local politicians and Armand's high-level enforcers, I left Eris working my way to Hil, Cali, and my mother.

"I think we have a problem," I said under my breath to Hil and Cali.

"I think you have a problem," Cali said no longer sober.

"Is it that a hillbilly is banging my brother?" I snapped back.

"Fuck you with that hillbilly stuff," Cali said drawing the attention of the people around us.

"Cali, you're a little loud," I said clutching his shoulder to make the conversation between us.

"Don't fuckin' touch me," he said sweeping my hand away. "You always think you can say whatever you want, do whatever you want. Well, I'm tired of it," he bellowed practically yelling.

"Calm down, Cali!" I insisted feeling everyone's eyes turn to us.

"Why? Because you say so. Then let me tell you what I say. I say that if you call me hillbilly one more time, we're gonna have a problem, right here, right now."

I couldn't believe what I was hearing. I looked at Hil amused. Immediately my brother knew what was coming next.

"Don't do it, Remy," Hil pleaded.

I turned to Cali ready. Violently poking his chest I said, "Listen here you inbred, banjo plucking hillbilly…"

That was when Cali snapped. Grabbing me like he thought he had a chance against me, I slipped my hand under his chin threatening to crack him open like a Pez dispenser. The two of us struggled back and forth until Lucien rushed over and broke us up.

As I waited for my chance to land my fist on Cali's jaw, Armand approached.

"Is there a problem here?" He said clearly pissed that we were fighting on his daughter's big day.

"Is there a problem?" Cali said turning to Armand. "Yeah, there's a fuckin' problem."

"Don't mind him. He's just drunk," Hil said putting himself between Cali and Armand.

Cali immediately swept Hil out of the way and got face-to-face with Armand. "You want to know what the fuckin' problem is?"

"I will warn you to watch what you say next."

"Cali!" Hil bellowed.

"You shot me. That's what the fuckin' problem is."

Armand looked like he wanted to rip Cali in half.

"I think it's time for you to shut up," Armand threatened.

"Look in my eyes. Do I look scared of you? Do you see anything familiar? Rattle loose any memories in that bat-shit crazy brain of yours."

Watching as Cali went off the rails, I backed off. His job in our plan was to create a distraction. We needed all eyes on him. He had refused to tell me how he was going to do it, which concerned me. But, he had done it. This was my chance.

As Armand's men slowly moved towards Cali, I slipped past them and up the stairs. Having the floor to myself, I hurried to Armand's office. Quickly picking the lock, I slid in. I had approximately 30 seconds before Armand's men dragged Cali outside and beat the shit of him. I needed to be back downstairs by then.

Pulling open the floor vent revealing the safe, I pulled out my phone. Retrieving the failsafe code, I entered it. In a moment, the safe popped open. Finding the two ledgers just as Jimmy had said, I pulled them out and flipped through them.

I couldn't believe it. This was it. And just as I was about to close them, the office door opened and someone stepped inside.

"Eris?" I said staring up into her cold, emotionless eyes.

"What are you doing?" She asked as if she already knew.

"It's not what it looks like."

"It looks like you, Dillon, your cousin, and your joke of a brother-in-law put this engagement party together to help you steal my father's accounting records."

I looked down at the ledgers in my hands at a loss for words.

"Would you believe me if I said I got lost on the way to the bathroom?" I said searching for my smile.

"You asshole! You made me believe that you were coming around," she said getting loud.

I quickly stood up and closed the door behind her.

"Look, you can't have me. Do you understand? I'm not a piece of property that you and Armand can just order around," I said dropping the charm.

"Well, we'll see what my father has to say about this," she said before trying to push past me to the door.

"I'm giving you a way out," I said, my voice rumbling.

"What?" She replied startled by my anger.

"These," I said holding up the ledgers. "These are your freedom. You don't want to marry me. You don't even know me. All I am to you is the best of a bunch of tragically horror options. You're only here because, like me, you're trapped. I take these and you have your freedom.

"You could meet someone who actually gives a shit about you. And you could have the life you so desperately want. You could be happy.

"Think about it. What would being happy for the first time in your life feel like? Tell me, Eris, what would it feel like?"

Eris looked at me in silence. The moment drew out long enough that I thought all was lost.

"It would feel good," she finally said washing my body in relief.

"Then, return to the party. Let me take this. And allow me to give Armand the justice he deserves."

"You can't," she said causing my heart to sink.

"I know my father's an awful person. I know he deserves everything you want to give him. But, he's still my father."

"Your father who is treating you like cattle."

"Being with you wouldn't have been a curse."

"But I love someone else, Eris. I love them with all of my heart. And I could never love you," I said gently.

Eris lowered her head.

"But, you can find someone who *will* love you. It just isn't me."

"I believe you. But you still can't put my father in jail. You can do whatever you need to to put an end to the two of us. But, if you put my father in prison, I would be left with nothing. I couldn't survive that," she said vulnerably.

Seeing the sincerity in her eyes, I realized that this was something I hadn't considered. I wanted to destroy Armand for what he had threatened to do to the people I cared about. But what would uprooting his thick, deep roots do to the ground left behind?

"Trust me," I told her knowing she had no reason to.

"How can I do that? You've betrayed me at every turn."

"What I did was fight for the man I love. Step out from in between us, and allow me to be your friend."

Eris stared at me blankly.

"Eris, one way or another, I'm going to leave here with these ledgers."

"Because you'll do anything for the people you love?"

"Exactly. And, what I'm asking is for you to trust me and become someone I can call a friend."

"Okay," she conceded before slowly stepping away from me and the door.

"Thank you," I said sincerely, seeing her in a new light.

Straightening myself up, I tucked the ledgers under my arm and exited the room. I was half expecting Eris to call her father as soon as I entered the stairwell, but she didn't.

And Cali was doing a much better job than I could have dreamed of. He was now just outside the open front door with Armand's men circling him. Hil was looking on like he was about to cry. And mother stood shocked.

With Armand still focused on the drunk country bumpkin making a scene at his daughter's fancy engagement party, Lucien raced to me to collect the books.

"Change of plan. I need you to take these, get out of here, and say nothing to anyone until you hear from me. Understood?"

"Got it," Lucien said taking the ledgers from me and rushing out the back door to the beach.

When he was out of insight, I turned my attention to the final part of our plan, stopping Armand from killing Cali. Pushing past the captivated crowd, I slipped between the men who circled Cali and stood in front of him. I held up my hands.

"Okay, everyone, just relax. The hillbilly's an asshole, but he's also very drunk. Tell them how drunk you are, Cali," I said looking back at the wild man behind me.

He looked at me with fury in his eyes. For a second I almost believed that this wasn't an act.

"I said, tell them how drunk you are, Cali."

Catching himself, he replied, "Really drunk."

I turned back to the crowd. "He's confused by any alcohol that doesn't come from a jug."

Someone in front of us snickered.

"Look, he's an embarrassment to me. He's an embarrassment to my mother. But, what can I say? My brother loves him. So, if I let anything happen to him, I'll never hear the end of it. Let's just end this with an apology and send him home to sleep it off."

When everyone looked calmer, I turned around. "Cali?"

"Yeah, where's my fuckin' apology?" he yelled at Armand.

"Okay, enough for you," I said turning Cali around and escorting him out.

"I want my fuckin' apology," Cali shouted over my shoulder.

"The show's over," I told Cali under my breath. "Rein it in, Dicaprio."

That seemed to register in his drunk brain. Looking me in the eyes before turning around, Cali continued to simmer as Hil, my mother, and I led him off.

No one questioned as I poured Cali into his truck. Nor did they say anything when I got in with them and drove off. Everyone knew we were from Manhattan. No one expected Hil or my mother to know how to drive.

Exiting the feeder road that led to the beach house, it wasn't long before a van with blacked-out windows pulled up behind us.

"Jimmy?" Hil asked staring through the back windshield.

"Jimmy," I agreed watching the van through the rearview mirror.

"Were they there?" Hil asked feeling free to speak.

"Was what there?" My mother asked, still in the dark about everything.

I peeked across the truck's bench seat at my mother.

"Hil's asking about what Cali just risked his life for."

"And, what's that?" She asked again.

"My freedom to be with Dillon."

"What?" My mother asked confused.

I smiled.

"So, was it there?" Hil repeated.

"I'm not sure yet," I replied remembering the pleading in Eris's eyes.

The four of us drove in silence back to my mother's place in the city. When we got there, poor Cali was even drunker.

"How many drinks did he have?" I asked Hil as we laid him onto my brother's childhood bed.

"He was nervous," Hil admitted.

"So, what? Eight? Nine?"

"Probably. Ten?" Hil said putting the waste bin on the side of the bed.

Staring down at Cali as he teetered on passing out, I felt for him.

"Hil, I'm only going to say this once. And if you repeat it, I'll deny I said it. But, Cali's a really great guy. You're lucky as hell to have him."

Hil smiled. "I know."

"Good job, bro," I said before wrapping my arms around my brother.

"You too, Remy," he replied, triggering more emotion in me than I expected.

Leaving Hil to care for his man, I entered the living room. Jimmy was waiting there with my mother.

"Mother, do you mind letting Jimmy and I talk alone?"

"Of course. Would you like another drink," she asked Jimmy.

"No. I'm good, thank you," he replied holding up his glass of lemonade.

When she was gone, I made myself a stiff drink and sat down.

"Don't leave me in suspense," Jimmy insisted. "Did you get them?"

I took a swig holding the alcohol in my mouth allowing it to burn my cheeks. Swallowing I said, "Kind of."

"Kind of? What does that mean?"

When my conversation with Jimmy was done, I knew that there was one more talk I needed to have. So, climbing into my father's now unused car, I drove back to Long Island. The security guard at the end of Armand's street looked pissed. Radioing that I was there, he got the go-ahead to let me in. My heart thumped.

I was expected to see Armand waiting for me at the front door. He wasn't. Entering the now darkened, empty house, I made eye contact with Eris who was there to greet me.

"Where is he?"

"Upstairs in his room," she said adding nothing else.

Jogging the stairs up, I crossed the hall to the master bedroom. With the door open, I walked in. Scanning the room, I found Armand on the balcony. He was staring out to the lightless beach. Knowing this was it, I joined him.

"You have them, don't you?" He asked not looking at me.

"I do," I said casually.

"How did you know they were there?"

"The FBI has been building a case against you for years."

"So, they told you."

"I know somebody," I admitted staring out at the beach with him.

"So what do we do now? Do I shoot your kneecaps until you give them back? Do I go after your family?"

"I wouldn't recommend it."

"Why not?"

"Because, right now, the FBI only has one of the ledgers."

"Which one?" He asked turning to me.

"The cleaned one, of course."

"And what, you're going to blackmail me?"

"It's a move I like to call, 'The Armand'," I said with a smile.

He chuckled.

"I don't take to blackmail as easily as you do."

"I imagine you wouldn't. But, I will remind you that right now, you have everything. Don't do anything stupid and that won't change."

"So, you're still going to marry Eris?"

"Oh, hell no. In fact, you're done with being involved with my life."

"So, you think you can treat my daughter like that and get away with it?"

"Why shouldn't I think that? You do."

"I'm her father."

"And her curse."

Armand laughed. "Maybe."

"Look, let's cut the crap. You don't give two shits about your daughter. The only thing you care about is what you've always cared about, your empire."

"You make me sound like a bad man," Armand said with a smile.

I laughed.

"Well, here's the good news. I'm going to let you keep your empire. The only condition is that you get the hell out of my life. And while you're at it, you'll stop trying to marry off Eris like this is the 1600s."

"Do I detect a soft spot for her?"

"What you detect is empathy. She doesn't deserve what you're doing to her."

"I'm doing it for her."

"You're doing it for you. Don't kid yourself."

Armand smiled. "Maybe I am. Let me tell you, it's hard to think they're precious when you have so many."

I wasn't sure what Armand was referring to but I didn't care.

"So, tell me, do we have a deal? Or do I take away your reason for getting up in the morning?"

Armand looked at me.

"Your father would be proud."

I didn't know how to respond to that.

"Do we have a deal or not?"

"We do."

"And you're gonna let Eris marry who she wants?"

"Only as much as any other father," he said looking at me with a smirk.

"Fair enough," I said knowing I had the best deal I could get. "Now, I hope to never see you again," I told him before turning my back to him and walking off.

Chapter 14

Dillon

My leg bounced anxiously as I sat on the worn couch in my New Jersey apartment. Staring at my phone, it didn't ring. It had been hours since I'd fled the beach house at Remy's insistence, and I hadn't heard a word from him since.

Waiting for his call, a thousand nightmare scenarios raced through my mind. Had something else gone wrong with the plan? Had Armand discovered what we were up to? Was Remy hurt? Was he dead?

When my phone rang breaking the silence, I nearly jumped out of my skin. The deafening noise bounced off the empty walls. Scrambling to pick it up, my hands shook.

"Hello?" I answered tentatively.

"Dillon, it's me," Remy said in a tone that instantly soothed my frayed nerves.

"Remy!" I cried. "You're okay! I've been worried sick. I didn't know what happened or—"

"It's alright," he said calming me. "Where are you? I need to see you."

"Is it safe to talk? How would I know if someone was forcing you to say this?"

Remy was silent for a moment.

"Remember that time when you were staying at my family's apartment and I walked in on you dancing naked with a hardon?"

Heat rushed to my face as fast as a nudist reaching for his zipper.

"I didn't have a hardon?" I protested wishing it weren't true.

"Okay. Whatever. Tell me where you are. I need to see you."

"I'm back at my place in New Jersey."

Just as I said it, someone knocked on my door.

"Oh my God, Remy. Someone's knocking at my door."

"Really? You should probably answer it."

"But what if…"

"You're gonna want to answer it."

I got up keeping the phone to my ear. Approaching the door slowly, I leaned in and looked through the peephole.

"Remy," I said flinging the door open and throwing my arms around him. "How did you know I was here?"

"I told you to go somewhere people wouldn't look for you."

"And no one goes to Jersey?" I asked sarcastically.

"Not willingly," he joked.

I laughed and swatted his arm.

"You came here."

"That just shows how in love with you I am," Remy said with a smile.

"You love me so much you're willing to come to Jersey."

"It's a love song that writes itself."

I laughed. "But seriously, Remy, what happened?" I asked ushering him in and onto my couch.

"It's over," he told me as he stared into my eyes.

"Really? Armand's going to jail?"

Remy paused. "Weeeell…"

"What?" I asked feeling my heart drop.

"What I can tell you for sure is that there's nothing that can stop us from being together."

"Eris?"

"She's now on our side?"

"And Armand?"

"He's agreed to leave us alone in exchange for me not destroying his world."

"So, you blackmailed him?"

"Pretty much," Remy said proudly.

"And how does Jimmy feel about not being able to put Armand away?"

"He doesn't like it, but he thinks it's because he gave us faulty information. I told him that only the cleaned ledger was in the safe and I've made arrangements to give it to him."

"But, you found both ledgers in there?"

"I did."

"Is there a reason you didn't give Jimmy both of them?"

"It's because if there's one thing I know, it's that in this life, it's better to make friends than enemies."

"What do you mean?" I asked confused.

"It's a long story and I have a lifetime to tell it to you."

"So, you're saying it's really over?"

"It is."

"And there's nothing stopping us from being together?" I asked feeling a crackling build inside me.

"Not a thing," Remy said with a sparkle in his eyes.

"Then maybe we should…"

And that was when he kissed me.

Remy's lips were like fire against mine, igniting a blaze that consumed my entire being. His hands roamed my body hungrily as our kiss deepened and my heart threatened to beat out of my chest.

Needing to feel his warm skin against mine, I tugged at his shirt. Without breaking our kiss, he unbuttoned it and pulled it off. My hands explored the hard muscles of his chest and abs. Feeling them flex beneath my touch made my cock throb.

With growing urgency, Remy guided me backward through my small apartment until my legs hit the edge of the bed. I tumbled onto the mattress. Remy's powerful body pinned me down. His lips trailed kisses down my neck and along my collarbone making me ache for more.

Skillful fingers made quick work of my shirt, exposing my heaving chest. Remy's tongue flicked over one of my nipples before drawing it into his mouth. I arched up against him, gasping at the jolts of pleasure shooting through me.

Remy's hands slid lower, working open my pants and freeing my aching arousal. He wrapped one large hand around it, stroking it firmly as he continued lavishing my chest with attention. I was lost in ecstasy, my whole world narrowing down to Remy's touches.

With his lips trailing lower, my stomach quivered. I looked down to see him take my throbbing cock into the velvety heat of his mouth.

"Oh god, Remy!" I cried out, tangling my fingers into his silky hair.

He worked me skillfully with his lips and tongue taking me right to the edge again and again until I was begging for release. Sensing how close I was, he finally drew back. Looking down my body at him again, a devilish grin highlighted his handsome face.

Sliding back up my body, he kneeled above me. Clutching my hips and picking me up like I was weightless, he flipped me onto my stomach. Tugging my hips again, he lifted me onto all fours.

Knowing what was coming next, I trembled in anticipation. His large, strong hand rode the muscles of my back. Stopping at my shoulders, he followed the angle down my arm. When his hand was on top of mine, his chest was pressed against my back. And with his free hand parting my cheeks, I felt the thick head of his cock nudging at my entrance.

Slick with precum, in one powerful thrust he buried himself to the hilt inside me. As much as my hole had opened wanting him, I ached. A wave of painful pleasure overtook me and I moaned.

I had forgotten how big he was. And when he gently pulled back and found my depths again, my legs wobbled. I was losing myself.

"Yes, Remy, please… harder!" I heard myself say.

He immediately complied. With deep strokes, he fucked me relentlessly. As the sound of our clapping flesh echoed, I groaned. This was a new side of Remy. It awakened something within me.

"Harder," I begged until the bed frame rattled violently beneath us.

My mind swirled in a haze of overwhelming sensation. The entire world narrowed down to Remy's thick cock pounding into me. It claimed me completely. I wasn't gonna last long.

Slightly changing his angle, he hit my sweet spot. Electricity crackled through me. It pushed me over the edge.

When my climax exploded, it ripped through me like a bomb. Stars burst across my vision. My spasming hole clenched around Remy's thick cock. It was enough to drag Remy over the edge with me.

Curling his back, he howled in pleasure and filled me with everything he had. Empty and exhausted, Remy collapsed on top of me. When his weight tested my weakened strength, I fell onto the mattress.

Together we were a tangle of sweaty limbs. And with us both gasping for breath, he slid beside me. As he laid gentle kisses across my shoulder, I ran my fingers over his sensitive skin.

"I love you," he murmured, nuzzling me affectionately.

My heart swelled, overflowing with emotion. This was only the beginning for us, but I knew then that I would never let him go. It felt like a lifetime that it had taken us to find each other. Now, here we were, together.

"I love you, too," I said crawling into his arms.

"I'm never going to let go of you again," he told me pulling me tighter.

I believed him. Remy was everything I ever wanted and everything I ever needed. He was mine as much as I was his. And lying there with his comforting warm breath enveloping my naked body, I knew that the two of us were going to live happily ever after.

Epilogue

Cali

Waking up the morning after Remy's engagement party, I felt like crap. Considering how much I had to drink, I was surprised I had woken up at all. I never drank that much and I knew I shouldn't have last night.

Hil thought my drinking was about liquid courage. In a way, he was right. But it wasn't the courage to act like the distraction Remy's plan required. It went far deeper than that.

Months earlier, Armand had kidnapped Hil. He had felt the need to shoot someone before he let Hil go, so I let him shoot me. Despite it being in the leg, I hated him for it. If I could have, I would have ripped off his head for what he had done to Hil and me.

But that was before I returned home and reconnected with my newly found brothers. During our next call together, Claude shared surprising news. For months, we had been trying to get anything we could from our mothers about the father we shared. It turned out that Claude had gotten his name.

When I read it, Claude asked if I had recognized it. I told him that I hadn't. But that wasn't true. I had.

Our father's name was Armand Clément. The man who had shot me was my father. The woman Remy was being forced to marry was my sister. And because I loved Hil, I had agreed to help put my father in jail for the rest of his life.

I was dealing with a lot. The drinking was the only way I could go through with it. And seeing that we all weren't dead, I had to assume that the plan had worked. My father was now arrested and was being held by the FBI.

Had I made a mistake? I had no doubt that Armand was an awful, dangerous man. But considering he had not just won the heart of my very smart mother, but had done the same to my brothers' mothers, didn't that mean that there was once more to him? Was that side of him lost forever? If I had told him who I was, would he have had a change of heart?

It was too late now, but if I had to do it over, I would have done things differently. If he wasn't going to be locked up for the rest of his life, I would have told my brothers who he was. Instead of writing him off, I would have asked my brothers to help me connect with him.

Working together, we might have changed him. Remy had made him seem like he was beyond redemption but there was always a chance, wasn't there?

Anyway, that's what I would have done if Armand wasn't already in FBI custody. But seeing how comfortably Hil was sleeping beside me, I was sure the threat to his life had been removed.

If things were different, though... If I had a second chance to connect with my father, I was sure that the lives of everyone back home would change forever. If only I had that second chance.

*****

Sneak Peek:
Enjoy this Sneak Peek of 'Grumpy Boss Trouble':

Grumpy Boss Trouble
(M/M Romance)

By
Alex McAnders

HIL

As I pull into Snow Tip Falls, there is nothing about it that makes me want to stay. It's a beautiful small town, but if you stop running, your problems have a way of catching up with you.

But then tragedy strikes, and suddenly I find myself wanting to help. And when the person needing help is a chiseled football player with brooding eyes, dimples, and an endless desire to protect me, I'm reminded of the other purpose of my trip, to have a one night stand that finally rids me of my gay v-card.

I know why I haven't lost it yet. Guys confuse me. Cali isn't confusing, mostly because he doesn't say much. Maybe he'll be the one. And if I get his rippling, jock body wrapped around me, it will totally be worth the heart break that will follow when he finds out who I am and what I've done.

CALI

You know how some people are rays of sunshine that light up a room? That's Hil. Man, it's annoying. Annoying or not, it's not like I can refuse his offer of help if I want to stay in university, or on the football team.

It's not that he's hard to look at. That guy makes me think dirty thoughts.

And, it's not like he isn't the sweetest, kindest guy I've ever met…

Wait, am I falling for the stranger who showed up out of nowhere wanting to fix my life?

There's a reason I like to keep to myself. And as hot as Hil is, I'm not sure my heart can take being hurt again.

*****

Grumpy Boss Trouble

Reaching down, he took my hand. His warm flesh against mine sent a tingle that rippled through me. I wanted him. I'd never been more turned on in my life. But I also wanted to respect him. I didn't want to do anything that he wasn't ready for.

Because of that, I reeled in my desire. It nearly broke me, but I did. Still holding his hand, we entered the room. It was weird seeing Hil's stuff scattered around my familiar space. I liked it. I couldn't have guessed how much.

"Do you have to head back to campus in the morning?" Hil asked as he hovered around his travel bag. "Yeah. But I'll be back early to help Mama settle in."

"I'll make waffles."

"I would like that. I think Mama would enjoy that too," I said, starting to relax. "We should probably head to bed. I'm thinking it's going to be a long day tomorrow."

"Of course," he said nervously.

Seeing how nervous he was, only made me want him more. I wanted to hold and take care of him. I wanted to protect him. And whether or not I admitted it, I wanted to slowly push into him, listening to his light moans as I did.

I turned away when I began to throb. I didn't know how I was going to do this. It was taking everything in me not to race across the room, scoop him into my arms, and throw him onto the bed.

"What's the matter?" he asked, lightly wrapping his fingers around my bicep from behind.

I could feel his body heat. My heart thumped needing him. Did he know what he was doing to me? Could he know what his touch was about to unleash?
Read more now

Sneak Peek:
Enjoy this Sneak Peek of 'Serious Trouble':

Serious Trouble
(M/M Romance)

By
Alex McAnders

Copyright 2021 McAnders Publishing

'I could feel the heat of him on me. I could barely breathe. Parting my lips as my heart thumped, I needed to be closer.'

Imagine having to sleep inches from your crush but not be able to touch him because he's "straight" and has a girlfriend.

———

CAGE
With NFL scouts watching my every move, the last thing I should be thinking about is Quinton Toro, my awkwardly sexy, genius tutor who makes me think about breaking my headboard. I might fantasize about everything about him at night, but I've worked too hard for too long to slip up now.

But if it came down to having him or a career in the NFL, which would I choose? The answer should be obvious, right? Then why can't I get the lustful way he looks at me out of my mind?

I might be in trouble.

QUINTON
The problem with falling in love for the first time is that it makes you do crazy things like think you have a shot with the chiseled quarterback with rippling abs, who is not only focused on going pro, but is straight and has a girlfriend.

He is the one who insists we spend time together. That's got to mean he likes me, doesn't it? Why can't I figure this out?

And, how is he going to feel when he learns how much trouble comes with being with me? The only thing I can hope is that we can figure out a way to be together. But could we do it without me getting my heart broken again?

*****

Serious Trouble

I'm falling in love with Quin. I can't deny it. Even as I lie in the morning light not getting nearly enough sleep, all I could think about was how I could touch him like I did last night.

When I heard him place his hand on the bed between us, I sent out my hand in search of his. I didn't know if I should or if he would want me to, but I couldn't stop myself. I need Quin. I ache to be with him. I feel like I would go crazy without him. And to be so close without being able to wrap my arms around him was torture.

I was about to relieve myself of the painful agony when I shifted and something buzzed. When it did, I realized I was still half asleep because it woke me up. I knew the sound. It was my alarm clock. I had forgotten to turn it off.

It was probably more accurate to say that I wasn't foolish enough to turn it off. Ever since I had met Quin, getting eight hours were impossible. Even if I was in bed in time to do it, alone in the darkness was when I thought about him the most. So to have him here now was like a dream come true.

The alarm buzzed again. Oh right, the alarm. I didn't want it to wake up Quin.

Instead of letting it ring like I usually had to, I popped open my eyes and figured out where I was. I was on the right side of the bed. The alarm clock was on the left. I had to reach over Quin to get it.

Not thinking about it, I straddled the guy beneath me and hit the off button on the clock. With it off, I realized where I was. Although our bodies weren't touching, I was hovering above him. I froze and looked down. He was on his back facing up.

My God, did I want to bend down and kiss him. I was right there. He was so close. And then he opened his eyes.

I stared at him, caught. He smiled, or was it a blush?

"Good morning," he said in a raspy morning voice.

Looking at him, I relaxed.

"Morning," I said getting one more good look at him and then rolling back to my side of the bed. "Sorry about that," I told him.

"No, I liked it," he said smiling ear to ear.

"You liked the alarm?"

"Oh, I thought you meant…" He blushed again. "It was fine. Does that mean we have to get up? It's so early."

"I have to get to practice. It's a long drive."

"Okay," he said squirming his body adorably.

Watching him settle, I was about to get up when I noticed something. I had a serious morning wood situation going on. Sure, I was only too happy to show him my hard dick last night. But, I was so turned on by being with him that I had lost all inhibition.

After a night's sleep, as short as it was, I wasn't so bold. Yeah, I was still as turned on as all get out. But, we weren't getting into bed. We were leaving it. That made a difference.

"We could sleep a little while longer, right?" Quin asked facing me, his gorgeous eyes begging for me to hold him.

"You can, but I have to get up. The bowl game's on Saturday. This is our last full practice before it. I can't be late."

"Fine," Quin said disappointed.

Staring into his eyes I tried to think of the next time I could get him back here.

"Do you want to come to the game? Have you ever been?"

"You want me to come to your game?" He asked with a smile.

"Yeah. Why wouldn't I?"

"I don't know. I thought it might be your manly space or something."

"Manly space?"

"You know, a place for your girlfriend and all of your football friends to meet and do football things."

"First of all, the stadium seats 20,000 people. There's room for everyone. Second of all, Tasha hasn't been to one of my games in I don't know how long. You should come. That way you can see what all the fuss is about."

"I can see what all of the fuss is about from here," he said making my heart melt.

Read more now

*****

Made in United States
Orlando, FL
03 December 2024

54917137R00153